AFFAIR OF THE HEART

ℋ 'There's a pleasure in pain' ℋ

LAVINIA DASANI

www.laviniadasani.com

This book is a work of fiction and any resemblance to names, characters, actual persons, living or dead, places, locales or incidents either are the products of the author's imagination or are purely used fictitiously. To the extent that the covers and pictures go, models and free pictures websites were used.

Self- Published.

ISBN (pbk) #978-1-7339857-3-4

ISBN (ebook) #978-1-7339857-4-1

Printed in the United States of America

WARNING:

The following material contains graphic sexual content meant for mature readers. There are explicit E-rotic and S-ensuous love scenes which would most likely leave nothing to the imagination and doesn't hesitate in its description. The love scenes are high in volume and might contain fantasy material that some readers find objectifying. However, I will give a fair warning that there might be some gruesome details within the literature. With this literature being an E-rotic and S-ensous plus action, there are going to be graphic languages.

This is an entertainment literature and you've been warned of its potentially 'dangerous' contents in advance.

Proceed with cautious – Not for the faint of heart.

1

Coming back to the State, I had spent half of my adolescence and adult life in, after five years of living in a whole different State, busy building my life from scratch, I would have never imagined bumping into my mom, Elize Buar, mopping the dirty floor of a grocery store.

There was nothing wrong with the job. I've always respected any person, no matter their position or work status in life. My lovely mother has forever ingrained the teaching of respecting a janitor the same way I would respect a CEO of a bigshot company, and I am proud to say I have never failed in this particular department. However, seeing the woman who has raised me and my brother from nothing, in that grocery store was a rude surprise.

This woman began her life with pennies in her pocket and rose to the peak of the mountain by working her butt off to make sure my brother and I never lacked anything in our life. Despite being constantly busy, she was a model of what a hard working woman and mother combined as one should be like. Thanks to her, we lived a near to luxurious life, and her support has made us the successful person we are today.

Gawking at her like she had several heads, I couldn't come up with an explanation as to why this woman - whom I've seen hold pens for my whole life would be holding a mop.

"What are you doing, mother?" Finally managing to form words, I silently prayed she wouldn't reply with what was the most obvious answer, given our situation.

"Good evening to you too, daughter." My mother sarcastically responded. My lips slightly pulling up, I was pleased, my mom's sense of humour was still very much intact. It was, after all, embedded in her.

"Mother!" Pulling my poker face, I've learned to perfect throughout the years on the field, I maintained a serious expression.

"I'm working. I would think it would be obvious given the wet mop I am holding."

"One would definitely think so... But my question is why? - If you got bored after your early retirement, you could have found a better job that wouldn't harm your back and health in a split second."

Hastily taking the mop from her hands and directing her away from the 'station' she was cleaning despite her resistance, I brought her to the wood section of the store so we could have a more private chat.

"Because some people need good lodgement and food to survive, Angel."

Confused by her statement, I blinked several times.

"Excuse me?" Unbeknown to me, the guy hauling woods behind me loudly cleared his throat, clearly asking us to move out of his way.

Swiftly turning on my hips to shush the guy, I was yet again left dumbfounded, thunderbolt, even. "Dad?"

Back strained, the man turned towards me with snail speed. Shock waves washed over his face. His skin paled to an even whiter colour as the blood completely drained from his face. Clearly, he was not expecting to see me here either. But, unlike my mom, he was unable to maintain a straight face. My dad was, after all the emotional one in the family.

"OKAY! What. The. Fuck. Is. Happening. Here!?" Looking back and forth from my mom and dad, I spelt out each word.

"Language, young lady." My mom scolded instantly. - Perhaps she had forgotten I was no longer her little daughter. Heck, I had my own kid for crying out loud.

"To hell with language, mom. Tell me what is happening right now?"

"Life is happening, Angel. We can explain everything later. But for now, we are still on the clock, and the last thing I want is for both your dad and myself to get fired."

"The hell you are! There is no way I am letting you both work here! Where is Pete, in all of this? And why didn't he put a stop to this stupidity? - Actually, we'll discuss this issue once I drop you two home. For right now, pack all your stuff, you are not coming back here to work ever again."

"Angel, don't be crazy! We need this job to survive."

"What type of surviving are you talking about, mom!? Your son is a millionaire for Christ's sake. You should be travelling in luxury or at home watching TV right now. Not mopping the disgusting floor of some grocery store, much less be working. And let's not forget about dad, he is hauling wood for the store. This is not normal."

"We don't live with Pete anymore, love. He couldn't handle having us under the same roof as him, so we had no choice but to move out. And since most of our savings were spent on you and Pete, we are left with pretty much nothing." My dad calmly explained. Advancing towards me with leaden steps, my dad, Auden Buar, placed both his hands on my shoulder blades, instantly making me less irritable.

Unlike my mom who had way too much pride to accept the fact that her dearest son kicked her out of his home without providing them with the necessary resources, my dad didn't have a bone of overconfidence in him. Oddly enough, his reluctance to boast and capability to be so grounded as well as speaking his mind without much filter made the relationship between him and my mom work like a pair made in heaven.

"Excuse me, but what!? - When the fuck did all of this happen? And why was I not informed?"

"It's been a few months now." Was my mom's only answer.

Shrugging at me as if it was no big deal, I was irked by her atti-

3

tude. - How could she be so calm? - I would have raised all hell if I were in her place. Or better yet, I would have called my eldest kid to ask for help or at least keep her informed of the situation. But hey, that's only what I would do.

My mom, apparently, would prefer to stay quiet. To keep me uninformed and restart from the bottom-up once again in her old age. This realization and situation seriously made me want to punch someone hard, and by someone, I especially meant Pete Buar, my millionaire and now apparently selfish brother.

"Just give me a sec to recapitulate and wrap my head around this -" Slicing my hands through the air, "Whatever this is."

Trying my best to not dramatize the situation no matter how mad I was, I momentarily shut my eyes, took slow deep breaths and counted till ten in my head. It was a neat trick I've learned in my field of work to calm my nerves. It works so beautifully, I even use it at home with Kyle Henry, my son.

"So mom, dad, you are telling me you've both moved back to your old place, been living there for the past few months and didn't deem it necessary to inform me of the misadventure that has taken place. You haven't found it important to let me know how selfish my dear brother has become after winning his millions in the lottery. What did you think, I would never find out?"

Arctically glaring at them, I felt a sense of disappointment washed over me. A disappointment at my own blood; my brother and at my parents. We used to be so close, loving on each other like no other and now look at us. I had to find out the truth about their situation like this.

"We didn't tell you because we didn't want to worry you. You had your own busy life in Miami. Plus we figured Pete would soon come to his senses and realize the mistakes he has made. So, why worry you when going back to Pete would soon be an option."

"Mom dearest, the last thing I want is to snap at you. But your logic infuriates me, to put it mildly..."

"Angel, listen to us and try to see it from our perspective." My dad effectively jumped in, rescuing my mom from my wrath.

"I will do all the listening once we are out of here. Pack up, I am driving us back home, no discussion." Standing my ground, my gaze locked, I challenged them to defy me.

"You don't understand, Angel. If we leave with you right now, we will get fired, then what? Have you thought further than this current moment? Besides, we don't own the family house anymore, we had to sell it for money. We rent an apartment in Broadway now."

Stupefying the life out of me, the blood drained from my face as my head began to throb. Blankly staring between my parents, I was stumped. I couldn't start to believe the words that just came out of my mom's mouth.

"Okay, I am done! You are both coming to Miami with me. I don't care what your logics are or this job you have here." Swallowing my anger like a bitter pill, "And if you want to continue waiting for Pete to recognize his mistakes, you can do so at my place."

Grabbing hold of their hands, I left no room for discussion and tugged them with me to the front counter of the store.

"Angel, you are being irrational." My mom tried once more in an attempt to resist me. Then again, she soon realized there was not much she could do at this point other than let herself be dragged.

"This is the perfect picture of rationale you've probably seen in a while, mother. - Dad, talk to her, please. I am going to let the front desk know you both are not working here anymore." Determination and authority flashing in the depths of my eyes, I was a bulldozer in the store. A bulldozer with a mission in mind.

"Excuse me, ma'am, I just wanted to let you know that Auden and Elize Buar won't be working here anymore."

"If they've done anything to offend you, ma'am, we will take it to the manager, but I can't just fire them for no reason." The woman, who appeared to be the assistant manager of the grocery store answered with professionalism and curiosity.

"With all due respect, ma'am, they've done nothing wrong. They are my parents, and I just found out they've been working for your store for a few months now. I got nothing against your grocery store, but I simply can't have my retired parents bust their asses here when they should be relaxing." Explaining my situation to the lady in a surprisingly calm manner, I killed her curiosity in a flash.

"Oh...." She muttered, the surprise and confusion in her voice as bright as the sunshine during summer.

"Yes, oh." Maintaining my professional composure, I nod at the woman before turning on my heels.

Marching towards where my mom and dad were busy discussing the new situation they were basically forced into by yours truly, I prepared myself to fight them until I win this battle. It wasn't a matter of pride for me. Oh no, it was a matter of love and respect. They had given everything to make sure Pete and I were well fed and taken care of, and now that they were older, it was my duty to make sure they were being taken care of.

I recognized forcing them to live with me in a whole different State where the sun instead of the rain kisses us almost every day of the year was harsh, impulsive and well, not a totally well-thought solution to the problem. But I could care less. I knew I would be able to make it work despite not owning a mansion for a home as Pete does.

I was well off myself. A renowned Cognitive behavioural psychologist, who also works in partnership with the State law enforcement when they require my excellent sense of observation and profiling. I bought my own suite in a protected 'rich environment' complex barely outside the outskirts of the city. And in my opinion, it is one of the best locations. I get to be in the city within minutes, yet be away from all the buzzing noises that come with cities. Furthermore, we have a large patch of verdure behind the main building complex with a mountain view, giving Kyle plenty of room to play outside with other kids, and for me to relax under the sunshine, by the pool.

Not to forget Anastasia, who is my best friend, helper and babysitter would be of great help. And if my parents still don't like the arrangement I would be providing them, I could always buy a home for them wherever they want and make sure they are well taken care of. If my mom wanted to keep working after all of my help, she better get into crocheting or some type of artistic ventures. Or even go travel for all I care.

"You guys are not changing my mind, and even if you try, I already got you fired." Stopping short in front of them, I matched my mom's challenging gaze and acknowledged my dad's com-

6

passionate expression.

"I can always find another job." My mom retorted.

One could always count on Mrs Elize Buar to challenge people for the pure fun of it. It was a sick sense of humour she possessed, but one I have grown to love throughout my lifetime.

"Honey, behave." My dad playfully warned my mom, at which she simply rolled her eyes.

Their bickering and teasing were for sure music to my ears given the shock therapy I went through in here after landing in this State only a day ago for business purposes.

"If you guys are done fooling around, let's go pack up all your belongings. My company's private plane will be leaving for Miami in a few hours."

"Aye, aye, Captain." My father jocularly responded in an attempt to lighten the mood.

Smiling up at him, I marched forward with them trailing behind me like discipline soldiers. Having worked closely with the police force and with all the disturbed, aggressive or even psychopathic individual that comes with it, I have mastered the talent to keep my composure in the toughest situation possible. Yet, as I drove to my parents' small apartment on Broadway, my blood was boiling, and my composure was cracking.

Not even my father's dumb jokes could calm the anger within me. A wave of anger undeniably mixed with confusion and disbelief. The reality that my brother, Pete, of all people, could act in the way they've described in the limited time we were driving up to their place was truly mind-blogging. In that small space of time, the perfect picture of my charitable, loving, forgiving and respectful brother was shattered into millions of pieces.

I had come back to visit my family with the utmost courage and expectation after having run away five years ago, and I am forced to leave here without even seeing a sight of my brother. A brother I was longing to see from the most bottomless pit of my heart. However, I knew if I were to see him right now, I would explode and end up being on trial for murder instead of acting as an expert advisor and profiler for the court system.

I had left this State after my disastrous marriage five years ago and never once looked back. I worked my butt off in Miami to reach the height I currently possess. Just as my mother, I hustled without complaining but instead tried to find the new positives in my life with my son by my side.

Albeit being a single mother was the scariest thing I have ever done in my life, I recognize in a heartbeat that I wouldn't be so far ahead in my life without my son. Kyle has been my pillar on so many occasions, and despite being only five years of age, he was a wise little thing. He, without a doubt, took after his grandma.

Waiting for the plane to take off, I was secretly glad my parents were finally going to physically meet Kyle and pamper him as any loving grandparent should. Despite the guilty feeling trying to thoroughly wash over me, Kyle deserves to spend time with his grandparents and if this is how it can happen, then so be it.

"I can practically see the wheels turning in your head, Angel, what's up?" My father's gentle teasing tone brought me back to reality.

"Nothing much." Granted we would soon be over the oceans, flying in this small can that we call a plane, it would be utterly stupid of me to bring up any sort of conflicting conversation. The last thing I wanted was to be stuck mid-air with a giant elephant in the room.

"So, you are just trying to make sure the plane's motor is running smoothly by furiously turning those wheels inside your head?" My mom nonchalantly voiced out, propelling me to raise an eyebrow at her and her attempt at jokes.

"We don't want the plane to crash on us after all." Returning back the joke, I taunted her with a slight smirk.

"Girls, the plane motors would be absolutely fine. Now, Angel, if you would please answer my question - with seriousness."

"Way to be a party-pooper dad..."

"Angel." His definitive final tone told me he needed an answer, probably for his own peace of mind.

"I was just thinking of Kyle, dad. I haven't had the chance to tell him anything yet, but he would be so excited to physically see

8

you both for the very first time."

"I am excited to see the little one too. He always seems so energetic on camera."

"Don't worry mom, you will get to feel all those energies to the point where you will start asking him to mellow down..... Just a warning to you both, Kyle is a MAJOR hugger. So don't be surprised if he jumps on you."

"I think I would be able to handle a five years old boy. I've looked after you and your brother for several years, after all." Slightly smiling up at my mom before breaking eye contact with her, I remained quiet. The mention of my brother so casually after what he had done to them brought an immediate sour taste to my mouth.

The worst part was, I knew I could never hate my brother no matter how bad he screws up. Disappointed and furious at him, for sure, but hatred, never once.

2

Placing my forefinger on top of my full red lips, I signalled for my parents to stay still and quiet. Tactfully removing my house keys from the side pocket of my pale brown leather jacket, I called upon my 'ninja skills' and unlocked the entrance door as discreetly and silently as possible.

Taking into consideration that Kyle was with Storm during my absence it was extremely likely that Kyle was still pass out cold from playing too hard, eating a lot of unhealthy food and binge-watching movies, especially since today was a Saturday and the last thing I wanted was to make up my tired baby boy. Having worked in close partnership with Detective Storm Ives for the past 2 years, my son and him have come to develop a special bond, which in turn strengthen and tighten our friendship and partnership.

Thankfully for me, Storm had an early shift this morning, saving me from immediately having to explain to my parents why a man they've never spoken to, was sleeping in my house and looking after my son like a father would. Notwithstanding, after today, they will eventually learn about Detective Storm Ives, and no matter how much I would love to delay this reality from happening, there was no getting out of it. I am on a current case with the man and Kyle had gotten way too attached to Storm.

Barely getting the time to put down all the suitcases my parents and myself were carrying, a cyclone came crashing into me with full speed. Falling on my post-derrière, I secured the little tornado between my arms.

"How come this superstorm of mine is already up?" Taunting Kyle between waves of laughter, I kissed him on the forehead and cheeks.

"I missed you." Giggling in his little five years old voice, Kyle snuggled up on me.

"Good morning Angelica, sorry, I couldn't keep him from bolting to the door. The moment he heard your footsteps, he zapped out of my grasp." Anastasia greeted with a small smile.

In her late twenties, red hair up to her neck, playful black eyes, she was the picture of affection and kindness. Fresh out of nursing school, Anastasia was an absolute blessing to my small family. She effectively looks after Kyle during my absence, cooks when I am too tired to do so, and is a great friend. Now that she is out of schooling though, she would be able to spend more time than usual working for me, which is genuinely advantageous given I now have both my parents living with me.

"It's fine, Ana, we all know how energetic this little one can be." Rising to my feet and settling Kyle on the ground, facing Anastasia, I nodded at her with my own smile.

Silently looking behind me with a questioning gaze, Anastasia placed my parents, who up until now were quietly standing by the entrance, on the spotlight. Fully turning towards my parents, Kyle steered out of my hold on his shoulder "Grandma, grandpa" running towards my mom and dad, he screeched with excitement.

"Surprise!" Doing my best to tone down the uncomfortableness of the situation, I swiftly introduced my parents to Anastasia and vice versa. Filling in the impending awkwardness, I explained the new living arrangement to Anastasia while Kyle excitedly and loudly jumped up and down.

"A surprise, indeed." Looking between my parents and myself for one last time, Anastasia voiced out her astonishment at the sudden addition in family members.

Unable to avoid or ignore her cocked eyebrows, I nodded at her in acknowledgement and mouthed, "I'll explain later" so no one would be able to hear us.

Turning towards my parents, who were already busy being entertained by our young Kyle, "Mom, dad, follow me. I'll show you both where you would be staying until, well, you decide not too. The room isn't exactly made yet, so bear with me. Anastasia and I would help you both make it more like home once you've had some rest."

Walking past my bedroom which happened to be the very first room, my parents, Kyle and Anastasia followed me to the end of the east hallway to one of the spare guest rooms, about a few feet away from Kyle's room.

"Thanks a lot, sweetheart. I truly have no words for how amazing you are. You leave me mouth agape with happiness. And don't worry about having to help us set up the room. You've brought us so far and are doing so much for us, we don't want to abuse your kindness and time." Standing inside the light beige room, my dad managed to make me happy and angry at the same time.

Receiving the loud affirmation that I was still a great daughter despite my many defects and wrong steps was amazing. However, listening to him insinuate he might be a burden to me when I literally had to drag his, and my mom asses here was hurtful. I recognized it wasn't necessarily his fault for thinking or talking as such, which made it so much harder for me. In that moment, the reality that my own blood-related brother was responsible for all of this hit me harder.

Deep down, I really wanted to teach that asshole of a brother of mine a lesson he would never forget. But this approach of mine would inevitably hurt my parents, especially my mom, more. At the same time, there was no denying that my brother would perish if he ever shows me his face without any decent excuse and explanation.

"Dad, Mom, I am doing all this because it is my responsibility as your daughter and also because I want to. Pete doesn't know what he is missing out on, but trust me, I do. Heck, both Kyle and I know what it's like to not have the luxury of having your physical presence in our life whenever we want."

"Oh, sweetheart -" Taking hold of my dad's hand, I locked gazes with both my parents.

"No, for real dad. I am sorry for what has happened with Pete, but I am also truly grateful to have you both here with me after so many years of being separated. So please remove the idea that

12

you might be a burden to me. Treat this home as your own."

"I am almost always here to help out, as well." Anastasia butted in with enthusiasm and glazed eyes. Clearly, she was getting emotional, as well.

"Hey Miss Over-Emotional, don't forget you got other responsibilities as well." Teasing Ana, who gave me a mocking expression, we lightened up the atmosphere which had started to weigh on us.

"Oh, it's just University and little Kyle for me… that's my life…" Ana dramatically summarized, "Right, Kyle."

Messing with Kyle's mass of hair, Ana brought our attention back on my curious little Kyle, who seems quite interested in our discussion. Full brown eyes opened big like a saucer, Kyle's face was the perfect picture of an innocent child who was introduced to full-on real-life drama for the first time.

Bending halfway to my knees and looking directly at Kyle, "Hey baby boy, would you please go help Ana in the kitchen to make sure she makes an excellent cup of tea for mommy. I am really thirsty and tired."

Nodding his head furiously and energetically, Kyle clapped his hands in excitement and pretty much screech "Yes, yes" before running in the direction of the kitchen to wait for Ana to catch up to his flashing speed.

Turning towards my parents, "You guys settle in. I will be in the kitchen explaining the entire situation to Anastasia and spend some time with my son. But if you need anything, don't be afraid to ask either me or Ana. She might be a little too energetic in the beginning, but she is a lovely individual."

Studying me with a peculiar look, "Are you two…. you know… a thing…?" My mother all but questioned with uncomfortableness laced in her voice.

Gawking at her and her flushed face for a beat without any word, a cloud of awkwardness formed above our heads. Gawping between my mom and myself, my dad started to rub the nape of his head in uneasiness, not knowing what to do or say next. As my mom opened her mouth to say something else, I simply couldn't keep a straight face and cracked up like a lunatic.

Clenching onto my stomach while laughing my ass off, I tried my best to recompose myself and not look like I am having a laughing attack. "Oh, mother… jeez…" Venting myself and wiping a single tear from my eyes, "Gosh… I miss you… your sense of humour… God…"

"What's wrong with you?" My mom asked with caution and confusion. Watching me cracking up out of nowhere, probably giving her ideas to send me to the funny farm.

"It's your question, mom." Composing myself and taking a deep breath, "Anastasia is like a sister to me and an incredible aunt-figure to Kyle, not my girlfriend."

"Oh." Red as a beet, my mom, simply responded.

"Yeah, oh… The woman and I are best friends and know pretty much everything about each other's lives. But if you do have any questions about her, feel free to ask her or me. Just keep in mind that even though she lives in this house and works here part-time, she is out a lot and sometimes even gone for a few days."

Kissing both my parents on their cheeks, I turned in the direction of the kitchen, but just as I was about to turn the corridor, my mom surprised me.

"Angelica… I just wanted to tell you… I am truly sorry for being judgemental of you and your decisions five years ago. I regret not being there for you when you desperately needed me. But most importantly, I apologize for not calling you, much less informing you when we were facing hardship and didn't have a place to live. I understand my actions hurt you more than what I had anticipated."

Stirred and touched, I instinctively ran towards my mom and gave her a bone-crushing hug. Like my father, I was an emotional fool, and more times than none, I take pride in it. Many people, like my ex-husband, Dylan Henry, have tried to remove this character from my personality. An essential character which makes me who I am today. Thankfully, I also have my mother's resilience and stubbornness within me, which have helped in keeping my emotions alive.

"There, there…" Gently tapping on my shoulder like I was a crying baby, my mom truly seemed out of her element.

14

Letting out a small laugh, "Thank you, mom. This got to be the nicest thing you've said to me in years."

Cocking her delicate eyebrows at me, "In years... I don't believe I'm that cold to you, Angelica." Staring intensely into her eyes, she astonished me once again. My mom, Elize Buar, honestly thought and believed she was not that cold when her nickname literally is 'The Ice Queen'.

"Don't worry mom, all frozen blood turns warm in this house." Swiftly kissing her on her cheeks, a bright smile plastered on my face, "Just remember, unconditional love and respect is the magic trick in this house." Turning on my heels, I left my mom and dad to settle in their new home.

~~ | | ~~

Sitting at the counter like an investigator ready to grill the life out of me, Ana's fingers drummed on the counter-top, causing small ripple effect inside my cup of tea.

Unbeknown of the situation, Kyle stared up at me from his seat and began to excitedly recount all he and Storm did while I was gone. Smiling down at Kyle, I tried my best to keep my interest in him and in what he was saying rather than letting my attention be diverted by Anastasia's inquiring gaze.

"So mommy, do you wanna play lego with me, please?" The way and speed that kid jumps from one conversation to another were hilarious without any doubts. The very moment he was done telling me his life story during my absence, his next question came up, leaving little to no space for a breath in between.

Playfully ruffling Kyle's dark hair, "I would love to, baby boy. How about you go get everything ready while I have a private talk with auntie Ana? I will join you when I am done, okay." With a gentle smile, I sent an overly energized Kyle to the living room with his boxes of legos. With the amount of energy pumping through him, there's no doubt Storm spoiled him rotten with candy last night.

"I love Kyle, but finally! ... Now tell me all. What happened over there? How come your parents are here with us? Do you know how long they will be living with us? Where's your brother? Why didn't he come along? ... Wait! ... Should I be scared of your mother? I remember all the stories about her-"

"Calm down, girl! You're gonna kill yourself with all these questions." Laughing the memory of my brother's action away, I managed to keep myself calm and collected.

"It is your tardiness to provide me with answers that's gonna kill me; not my many questions. Keep me waiting, and I might start having a cardiac arrest." Throwing a piece of smarty chocolate at me from the glass bowl we keep on the kitchen counter, Ana had me cracking up at her childishness.

"Curiosity killed the cat, young woman. One would think you would be aware of the latter by now." Purposely dragging the conversation, Anastasia's impatience level rose even higher, making the situation all the more priceless and funny for me.

"Angelica Buar, I would like to remind you, your dear son is waiting for you, so out with the answers or you are staying here with me." Playing dirty, Anastasia quirked her eyebrows at me.

"You, my dear Anastasia Riles, are a major party-pooper."

Giving in her persistence, I recounted all I found out when I went back to my home State. Letting her know of my confusions, feelings and disappointment, I answered all of her questions. At least those I had an answer for.

3

Waking up from my late afternoon nap to the sound of Kyle's giggles and my parents' laughter from the kitchen area, I went to investigate what the whole ordeal was. I too wanted to know what could be so entertaining in the kitchen. Walking up to them at a leisurely pace, I was surprised by the view of all three baking cookies and little Kyle covered in flour from head to toe.

Taking in this messy yet beautiful, unfamiliar sight, I felt a gentle tug in my heart. The whole scenery playing in front of me was so surreal it almost felt like I was dreaming and still sleeping off the strain of my body from my flight back to Miami. And if all of this was indeed a trick of my mind, I did not want it to stop anytime soon. Particularly after hearing all of the shocking news about my brother and my parents' state of living.

"I wasn't aware turning my little Kyle into a cookie monster was part of today's schedule?" Approaching them with a smile, I cheekily commented while trying not to let the disastrous state of my used-to-be tidy kitchen affect this joyful moment.

Running towards me with another giggle, Kyle left a trail of flour behind him, "Grandma says not to call me a monster because I am an angel." Smacking his floury self into my legs, I bent down to Kyle's level knowing my clothes would soon need to go to the washer, just as his.

"Oh, really now." Raising my fine eyebrow at my mother then at Kyle, "Did grandma also told you that you aren't just any type of angel?"

Picking his curiosity, Kyle shook his flour-filled hair on my face. Immediately closing my eyes to avoid having to struggle from a sting-eyeball for the rest of the evening, I sputtered out the flour dust which got deposited on my lips. Gently dusting off my face, I softly ruffled Kyle's hair, removing the rest of the residual flour sitting on top of his head.

"You, my love, are mommy's personal guardian angel." Lightly wiping off the floury pasture on his cheek, I pressed a gentle but firm kiss on his cheek before getting back up on my feet.

Grinning brightly as if he has won the biggest lottery in the universe, "Yes! I am your guardian angel, mommy." Hugging my legs with more strength than before, "I love you, mommy." Kyle exclaimed with affection and true-to-God love before rushing back to my parents' side.

"Hey, what about us, young man?" My father inquired, faking hurt.

"I love you too, grandpa." Hugging my father's legs, Kyle professed with a small laugh, "You too, grandma, I love you." Moving to my mom's side, Kyle embraced her the same way.

"That's right, little one, share the love. – Hi mom, dad." Greeting my parents with a small laugh, I went to fill a pot of water, placed in on the stove and began preparing myself some tea.

"Hey, Angel, how was your nap?" My mom inquired while helping Kyle make the mould for the cookies.

"Good. It was much needed. I hope you guys got to relax as well." Standing by the stove, I turned to fully face all of them.

"We laid down for a while, but that's about as much relaxation as we could get in a new place." Letting Kyle play with more flour, my mom voiced out.

Silently nodding, I watched Kyle enjoying himself. My lips pulling into a smile, I was more than happy my little man was having a blast, particularly with people he hasn't physically met before today. Nevertheless, the thought of how much hassle and work it would be to get all those flour and sticky dough entirely off of him and his mane of black thick hair plague my mind. I wasn't, however, going to let my obsession for tidiness and control ruin this beautiful moment in my son's life.

"Your dear friend showed us around and let us know where everything was before taking off." Placing a batch of cookie dough inside the preheated oven, my dad added after a few beats of silence.

"I'm glad she did, and hopefully you guys got to bond with her in the process." Pouring the pot of steaming hot water into my favourite cup, with a scoop of sugar, a slice of lemon and a bag of mint tea, "Where is the woman anyways?" Walking to the front of the counter, away from the danger of flying flour, I asked both my parents.

"She mentioned something about needing to have a discussion with a certain Jackson." My mom nonchalantly pointed out.

"Jackson, huh!" I mumbled with a slight tint of disgust without thinking twice about it.

My tone and eye roll, however, got my parents' full attention and interest, more specifically, my mom. The control freak in her simply needed to know what was going on in her surroundings or who exactly was the people around her and the people involved in the life of the people around her. I'll bet my ass to a dominant right this instant that the uncertainty of this whole situation and this new environment was driving her crazy. I know it would for me and this aspect of me came directly from her.

"Why do you say his name this way?" My mom questioned, proving my point in a heartbeat.

"It's nothing, mom. It's just Jackson." I merely stated, doing my best to not give out any details about Ana's personal life, since it wasn't my story to tell.

"Mommy, isn't Jackson the name of the bad guy who made Auntie Anna cried?" Kyle inquired with utmost innocence, plain confusion washing over his face.

Facepalming, I exhaled out a slow breath, "Kyle, baby, what did I tell you about filters and intruding into other people's conversations." – I was NOT going to get mad at Kyle, I kept telling myself. The child was just trying to help out and understand his surroundings better.

"Are you mad at me, mommy?" Lowering his eyelids, Kyle asked in a small voice, the realisation he must have done something wrong dawning on him.

"Come here, baby boy." Keeping my hot steaming cup of tea on a small spot on the counter where it was flour-free, "I am not mad at you, Kyle. A bit disappointed you didn't take what we had already talked about into consideration, yes, but I know your intention was good, and that's all that truly matters to me. But next time, please think twice before you butt into someone's conversation, okay."

"Okay, mommy." Slightly nodding his small head, Kyle gave me a little peck on the cheek before running back to his grandparents' side.

"As for you, mom and dad, I wish I could tell you more, but this isn't my or Kyle's story to tell. If you want to know more, ask Anna."

"That's cruel but fair." Was my mother's only response before she turned her attention back to Kyle.

"Whatever it is or whoever this guy is, I hope Anastasia would be fine. She is a good kid, I can already see it. Not only does she love you and Kyle, but she is sweet, genuine and extremely hard-working." Staring into the depth of my eyes with actual concern and appreciation for Anna, my dad stated.

"I hope so too dad, I hope so..." Walking out of the kitchen, I muttered under my breath, but loud enough for him to hear me.

~~ | | ~~

Lounging on my couch with a blanket over my legs and a hallmark action movie playing on the big screen Tv in front me, I typed a quick encouraging and supportive message as well as a threatening message to cut off Jackson's dick if he misbehaved and sent it to Anastasia.

Blowing out the smoke from my cup of hot tea and slowing taking a few seeps, I lost myself in the movie. Surely Anastasia was going to be alright confronting the jerk that was Jackson on her own. The only possible scenario I should be scared of is Anna stumbling again and hooking up with the asshole in the heat of the moment.

Engrossed in my own thoughts, the movie playing as background noise blocking all sounds from around me, I easily zoned out the noise of the main door opening.

"Guess who?" Instantly brought back to reality, all the hair on my body rising to attention and my sight darkened, I placed my hand on top of the one hand covering my eyes.

"Storm." I didn't need to touch the guy to know it was him. I would easily recognise his voice anywhere. Not to mention he is the only guy who dares and is allowed to come this close to me.

His hot breath fanning over my neck, Storm removed his hand from my eyes, giving me my sight back. "Him in person." Pressing a firm long yet gentle kiss on my jaw, the top of my body instinctively pressed against his chest and my neck stretched to give his lips more leeway.

"I missed you." Kissing the side of my neck but quickly pulling his lips away, leaving my skin tingling and needing more, Storm used the back of the couch as support and jumped onto the sofa to sit beside me.

"I was gone for only two days, Storm." Smiling at the Caucasian dark-haired, pale green almost grey eyed, extremely well-built man with one of the most beautiful and sexy smiles I've seen on a man, I jocularly brushed him off.

This man knew he was hot beyond hell. Knew he was the catch. He even frequently works his body to make sure his muscular firm self doesn't lose its appeal and beauty. But most importantly, he knew I once had a major crush on him. Unluckily for both of us, just as we were about to go on a date to see if we as a couple could work out, his boss contacted mine to establish a partnership between us. And this was the end of us in that domain.

Not because it was against any rules, but because I sure as hell didn't want to take the risk to date someone I would have to work with on a continual basis. Especially with Kyle in the equation. The risk of broken hearts and significant hurt was too high to even contemplate, particularly when I've known from day one that Storm Ives is a renowned and proud playboy.

"Two days too many if you ask me." Bringing my reverie back on him and his smirk, I grinned back.

"Such a charmer you are."

Shrugging his shoulders at me, I noticed Storm was trying to hide something behind his back the whole time.

21

"What are you hiding?" Voicing out my curiosity, I tried to peak on either side of him from my seat, but he expertly moved it each time.

"Nothing." Acting surreptitious, Storm pretended he had no clue what I was speaking about.

"Oh, really now." Shifting closer to him, I pushed Storm down.

His back hitting the couch he laid still as I straddled him and attempted to snatch whatever he was hiding underneath him. Laughing and fighting him on the couch to the point where my blanket wrapped around my buttocks and stuck between his thighs, imprisoning us in its tangled mess, I successfully managed to seize hold of the bottle wrapped in a brown paper bag.

Cocking an eyebrow at him, "What is it?" I inquired with curiosity.

"I don't know … Maybe your favourite wine." Holding onto both sides of my hips, Storm ambiguously articulated. Making a mental note to **ignore** the sensation of his palm burning its warmth onto my skin through my cloth or his hard-on pressing onto my womanhood, I brought all my sensory emotion to the bottle in my hands.

"Go ahead, open it." Motioning for me to open the bag with a nod, Storm acted as if he didn't know I was aware of his pressing manhood on my entrance when in all reality, something this huge could not go unnoticed.

His plan to get my attention back to the bottle, however, worked and got me all excited and curious again, because God knows how much I needed a good glass of red wine. Opening the bag, I pulled out the bottle of wine. – My favourite and one of the most expensive red wines. Squealing like a little girl in a candy shop, I hugged the life out of him and laid a 'thank you' kiss on his cheek, while making sure the bottle of wine was way above his head. We didn't want any disaster, after all.

"I'm gonna guess your visit back home didn't go particularly well." Storm spoke against my ear, returning my hug with a firm squeeze.

"How astute of you." Grinning against his cheek, I sarcastically uttered.

22

Cough *Cough* *Cough*

Two distinct loud fake coughs separated Storm and me in a blink of an eye. In a cacophony of mess, I pushed myself off of Storm while he pushed himself off the couch and attempted to pin me down on the couch all at the same time, the blanket became a death trap around both of us.

Placing his knees on either side of me, Storm's mere body mass restrained me on the couch. Poking his upper body over the couch, Storm pulled his freaking gun on my parents. If they were surprised before, they sure as hell were shocked out of their mind now. Me, on the other hand, I was trying really hard not to be affected by Storm's member screaming its 'Hello' at me while being under him. The temptation to touch it was extremely heightened, especially with him pointing his gun at the 'intruders'.

"Who are you?" Looking up at my hero of the day, from my position, I sensed and saw his body tensed furthermore, and I knew he saw Kyle with them.

"Touch the kid, and I won't think twice before pulling the trigger!" His authoritarian cop voice which has always had the knack of getting me all hot and bothered, boomed inside the room of my suite.

Touching his belly to get his attention, "Not now, Angel." Storm swapped my hand dismissively, without removing his fiery glare from my parents.

"Storm! They are my parents, stupid."

Dismissing the idea of smacking his cock to get his utter attention, I pulled onto his shirt with more force, propelling him to fall on top of me. Hissing, in an attempt to hide the obvious moan that tried to leave my mouth when his hard member smacked into my already soaked entrance, I turned his attention to me.

"You okay?" Gun above my head, Storm asked with concern.

Simply nodding my head, I took a deep breath to get myself and my hormones under control. I was a big girl, after all, not a teenager.

"Get that hard-on under control before you move too much." I hissed under my breath, not wanting anyone to hear us.

I was pretty sure my parents have been watching us from the very moment Storm opened my damn door, and the last thing I wanted was for them to see Storm's cock poking through his pants or our desire-filled eyes. Besides, I absolutely do not trust myself to be able to maintain control when he and his every part are this close to mine.

"Oh …" Looking down at me and staring back up at my parents with embarrassment and awkwardness, Storm turned bright red.

"Yeah, oh," I said in my normal voice with a small laugh.

Leaving a few beats for both of us to get a hold of ourselves and our genitals, "Care to get off me now." I mocked, raising my eyebrows at him.

"Shit … yes … sorry …" Scattering to his feet like an idiot, Storm patted down his clothes, more specifically his pants and put his handgun back in his side holster.

Stepping towards my parents with utmost carefulness, "I am so very sorry, Mr and Mrs Buar." Stretching his hands towards my parents, "I am Detective Storm Ives." Storm introduced himself with a smile, polite as ever. A politeness I've never seen from the man before. Not even when he had to break the news of death to an already grieving mother who we also had to question on the spot.

Shaking his hand with reserve, both of my parents eyed him with curiosity and wariness. "Auden Buar; and this here is my wife, Elize Buar." Seizing him up, my father finally introduced after a long awkward beat.

"Again sir, I sincerely apologise for my actions. I wasn't aware Angelica had company tonight, or I would have never been so jumpy at unknown voices coming out of nowhere."

Oh, so now I was Angelica to him, all of a sudden. – What magic trick was that? From the very first day we met, he had nicknamed me, never using my full name unless he was beyond angry, which is like a .1 per cent probability with this guy despite my several attempts to anger him. In the two years, I've known him, there was only one time he was beyond piss with me for not obeying his order and going right into the den of the lion while investigating a gang murder. He has always addressed me as Angel, Ang, Doc,

24

Mommy when he is speaking with Kyle about me or sometimes even Miss Know-it-all, especially when I frustrate him, or when we are playing around.

Placing the bottle of wine on the round glass table in the middle of the living room, I walked up to Storm.

"You are rambling, Mister." Smirking up at him, I mused, finding his discomfort more than funny. Throwing me a daggered look, Storm clearly wasn't as amused as me.

"Storm, I made cookies. Grandma and grandpa taught me how to." Leaving my parents' side, Kyle broke Storm's daggered glare towards me and hugged his legs.

"Is that right, young man?" Bending down to his level, Storm high fived Kyle.

"Yes, it is chocolate chips. Come, I'll show you." Taking Storm's big hand in the small of his hand, Kyle waited for Storm to get back on his feet before dragging him inside the kitchen.

Following the two boys, I feign not noticing my parents piercing intrigued questioning gaze. The intensity of it able to drill a hole on my back.

Pointing at the oven glass, Kyle showed Storm his chef-d'oeuvre in the making.

"It looks delicious Kyle. I can't wait to try it." Stopping his hand midway, Storm entirely took in Kyle's floury self.

"What happened to you, young man? Were you trying to turn into a ghost?" Smiling at Kyle, Storm taunted.

"Mommy said I am her personal guardian angel. And angels are snow white." Cracking a laugh at Kyle's theory and explanation, I joined the two boys in front of the oven.

"Is that so?" Looking at me as I stood beside him, Storm voiced with interest.

"This guardian angel of mine needs a real good hot soapy bath. – That's what he needs."

"Noo … I won't be as white as an angel then." Whining, Kyle stepped away from me. I swear one of these days the cuteness of this boy would be the end of me.

Crunching down to his level, "I'll let you on a little secret, Kyle, but 'shush' don't tell anyone else, okay." Storm baited Kyle.

"Okay." Was Kyle's only response as he leaned closer to Storm with inquisitiveness.

"I'm your mommy's guardian angel too. But you see, I am all showered up, clean and non-floury."

Oh, really now. I wasn't aware that I had two guardian angels in my life, but whatever, I better bite my inner cheek and remain silent.

Lowering his voice to a bare whisper, "Are you really?" Kyle asked for confirmation.

"I swear." Fist-bumping Kyle. Storm got Kyle all wrapped up in his words.

"How about that shower then?" Butting in, I inquired with raised brows.

"Can Storm help you with the shower again, please mommy."

Laughing at Kyle's little jump, "You gotta ask him for that baby boy, not me." Pointing at Storm, I let him make the decision. The last thing I wanted was to make Storm do something he doesn't want to.

"I would love to." Standing to his feet, Storm stretched his hand out for Kyle to take.

"Doc." Handing me his gun to put in my personal safe, as usual, I took it from the grip.

"You guys get going. I will put this away, get a towel and a set of PJ."

"Mommy can Storm choose my PJ after the shower, please."

" Alrighty then, Storm's little follower. As you wish."

"Thank you, mommy." Walking past my parents, hand in hand with Storm, Kyle was unknown to the tension in the room. Or better, simply choose to ignore it. Acknowledging my parents with a nod, Storm quietly followed Kyle to the bathroom.

Waiting for them to be out of direct earshot, "Mom, Dad, I know you got tons of questions, and I promise to answer them later on.

But right now, I have to take care of Kyle." Avoiding prolonged direct eye contact with both of my parents, I attempted to walk past them after making myself clear.

"Just tell us if he is your boyfriend before you run away?" My mom inquired; or better yet, demanded the very moment I stepped past them.

"No mom, he is not." I simply uttered, aware this was going to be the first and foremost question they would have.

Entering the bathroom, I sat down on my knees beside Storm, joining him with splashing water at Kyle. Convulsing with laughter, Kyle played with the bubbly water. Diving into the pool of steaming water every now and again, Kyle helped in removing the dough and flour from his small body.

"Do I need to guess what the main question you're parents asked before you joined us?" Locking his gaze with mine, Storm inquired while Kyle played with his cars and trains in the tub.

"The usual. – Whether we are dating or not?" Shrugging my shoulders, I answered back. At this point, it was no big deal. Everyone we meet, initially think me and Storm are a couple. There was no battling it and no changing how we behave towards each other.

"Figured as much. But hey, at least they didn't see my erection for you." Lightly hitting me on the shoulder with his broad shoulders, Storm stated in a low voice for only me to hear, his infamous smirk playfully decorating his face.

"Do you seriously think they didn't notice that huge thing? They are my parents, Storm." I stated in a 'duh' tone, draining all the colour from his face.

"Shit!" Absentmindedly playing with the pool of water in front of him, Storm's nervousness nearly cracked me up.

"Storm, mommy, look at my car driving on top of the water." Grasping our attention once more, Kyle made engine-starting noise through his mouth while demonstrating his magic.

"That's cool man. What else can it do? Can it fly?" Playing along, Storm welcomed the distraction and gave Kyle his undivided attention.

Taking in this lovely sight in front of me, I could not help but smile. Seeing these two like this tugged at my heart every single time, feeling me with utter happiness. Our moments were, however, short-lived. Feeling the stares of my parents on my back, it dawned on me they've silently and surreptitiously been watching and hearing us once again.

"Can you sense them?" I whispered for only Storm to hear. Kyle was too interested and vested in his water games to pay any real attention to our mummers or us.

"I can literally hear their questioning gaze, Ang. And my stupid move when they faked a cough hasn't helped my case either." Storm explained in an equally low voice.

Reaching for his arm, I gently squeezed, "I appreciated your stupid move." With a slight smile, I tried to ease his discomfort and anxiousness.

"If my memory serves me right – and it rarely ever does anything but- you snickered at me, not show your appreciation." Faking hurt and turning his gaze away from me, Storm complained in a low voice.

"Would me kissing my hero show enough of my appreciation and grant me his forgiveness, Your highness?" In a low suggestive tone, I once again caught Storm's undivided attention.

"That could be arranged." Briefly looking at me before turning his attention back to Kyle, Storm playfully stated.

Leaning towards him, I allowed my breath to linger on the side of his cheek and neck. "Alright then," I whispered with a hint of flirt. Closing the distance between us, I pressed a lingering kiss on his cheek and pulled back to return to my original position at the sight of Kyle curiously gazing at us before shrugging his shoulders and returning to his toys.

"Am I all forgiven now?" I cheekily inquired, aware this small not-so-innocent act of mine turned Storm on. We might very well be just friends, but I know all the buttons to push to get him all riled up.

"I have no choice but to." Storm mumbled after getting a handle of his composure.

"Mommy, I'm done with my bath." Standing butt naked in the tub of water, Kyle captured our ultimate attention.

"No, sweetheart, you are not. You still need to be scrub." Chuckling, I pulled Kyle towards me.

"Would you pass me the sponge, please." Sitting Kyle back down on his butt in the warm soapy water, I waited for Storm to hand me what I needed. Rubbing and sponging Kyle while making sure he keeps his eyes shut, I clean every single part of the boy.

"Storm, would you please help me get dressed? Mommy makes my hair look weird."

"Hey there," I exclaimed with a mock appalled.

Ignoring me, Kyle got his way and lifted his hands for Storm to pick him up. Handing Storm the towel, I let him dry Kyle and hold him in his embrace. Having been with us for so long Storm knew Kyle loved cuddling and being held after a shower.

"Tell me about it, young man." Teasing me, both of them got a nasty look from me.

"Don't worry mommy, we still love you." Cuddling against Storm's broad chest Kyle seeps in Storm's warmth.

I knew exactly how that boy felt. There was just something about Storm's cuddle and embrace that's warm, comforting, safe and addictive.

"Yes, mommy, we do." Ruffling Kyle's hair, Storm voiced out on his way out of the bathroom with Kyle in his arms, causing an immediate halt on my steps.

Wide eyes and a heart beating rapidly and out of sequence, I surely must be overthinking his words. Storm surely couldn't mean his words the way I am thinking. No, he must mean it in a friendly way. – Yes, it must be that.

"Are you coming, Doc?" Calling me from Kyle's room doorstep, Storm brought me back to the present.

Inhaling a deep breath and exhaling out my nervousness, I convinced myself I was merely overthinking the whole situation. It must be my parents being here and all.

"Yes, coming," I called out before joining them.

Catching a glimpse of my parents patiently waiting for us a few feet away, I threw them a shy smile. Clearly, they saw and heard pretty much everything that happened inside the bathroom given the door was opened.

Walking inside Kyle's room, Storm had already finished dressing Kyle up in a set of Spongebob PJ and was on his way to help him choose a game. "Are you choosing your game for the night, Kyle?"

"Yes, mommy."

"Would you please make sure you are choosing the ones you can play by yourself. Mommy, Storm, grandma and grandpa need to have a long talk without any disturbance before dinner time. Do you think that's possible, sweetheart?"

"Can Storm play with me next time, though?" Kyle asked with expectation.

"Of course, big boy. I'll play and beat you at the same time." Storm interjected.

"Okay." Accepting my conditions without any fuss and excited at the idea of being able to beat Storm on their next game, Kyle ran to the living room with his Xbox cart game CD in hand.

"You're ready for the million questions and intense interrogation?" Looking up at Storm, I asked with a deep intake of breath.

"As ready as I'll ever be." Taking my hand in his, Storm laid a gentle kiss on the back of my hand before we stepped out of Kyle's room.

4

Helping Kyle install his game on the large screen TV, I sat him down on the carpeted floor with his controller in hand and headset on. Aware I couldn't push the inevitable any longer I took my seat beside Storm on the couch, facing the other sofa my parents were impatiently occupying.

"I can literally sense the trillion questions boiling inside you guys. So how about you converse between you two then ask your questions one by one before either of you starts erupting like a volcano." Attacking the massive elephant in the room head-on, I spoke up to both my parents.

Intently studying Storm and me and our close proximity, my mom and dad silently nodded their heads. A silence capable of slicing us into pieces. Whispering between themselves for what felt like forever, Storm looked down at me as I look up at him with a hint of anxiousness and nervousness. The wait was slowly killing both me and Storm.

"Detective Ives, how about you for starters. Tell us how you know our daughter and for how long?" My father professionally demanded, his usual jocular demeanour and tone vanished into thin air.

Anyone who would look at my father right now would never ever guess or believe he is one of the most kind-hearted, open, caring and genuine men. At that moment, he resembled my mother; cold, standoffish and distant, shocking me. It was the first time I've even seen my dad this serious. Heck, he wasn't ever this serious and stoic when questioning my ex-husband, Dylan Henry, about his intentions when I brought him to my parents' home for the first time.

"Please call me Storm, I insist. To answer your question, I've known Angelica for about 3 years now. And given your daughter is one of the best cognitive behavioural psychologist, analyst and profiler in this entire State as well as the only woman who's been able to put up with me for more than a few months, our bosses deemed it necessary to have us work together. I work with the State law enforcement on special circumstances criminal case as the primary Detective. We can't divulge too much about our pro- fessional relationship or what it is we do, but if you should know, Angelica uses her expertise and talent to assist me as my primary partner."

"We've officially been working together for two years now." I jumped in, cutting Storm's extensive praising short. I get he was trying to impress my parents, but it really wasn't necessary. We were both adults, and my parents couldn't break our friendship even if they tried. We were just explaining ourselves as a courtesy and a sign of respect.

"Two years and 3 months actually." Turning towards me, Storm corrected me as if the exact time mattered.

"Why don't you tell me the exact day, minute and seconds while you are at it." My tone laced with sarcasm, I defied Storm.

Looking down at his watch, Storm remained silent for a few sec- onds, "Two years, 3 months, 8 days, 33 minutes and 50 seconds from today."

Mouth agape like a fish in desperate need of air, I gawked at Storm, baffled and out of words. The man was impossibly frus- trating sometimes.

"I'm glad you know the exact time, Storm. Now tell me, you two are only work partners?"

"Mom! I told you earlier, we are not dating." Somewhat annoyed by her incredulous gaze, I exclaimed with exasperation, not giving Storm the chance to speak.

"I'm speaking with the man, Angelica, not you. Sit quietly until your turns come." Flashing me an icy glare that I returned with a fiery one, my mom tried to dismiss me.

Resting his big warm hand on top of mine, Storm calmed the fire within me in seconds. Truly speaking, I didn't have much against

32

my mom and her prying questions, I was simply exhausted from always having to fight people about my relationship with Storm. Yeah sure, I would totally let the guy make love to me and date him if I wasn't such a scaredy-cat with a wall as high as the length of China wall. But the latter wasn't the case now, was it.

Linking his fingers with mine and ignoring my parents' eyes following his every movement, "Our relationship is far more than just work partners, Ma'am. I'm sure you are mainly referring to Angel's and I's behaviour when I first came in tonight, but I assure you, Ma'am and sir, our relationship is platonic. Working in the field together, our lives literally depend on each other, which requires a tremendous amount of trust and honesty. The two of us are exceedingly close because of this, but at the end of the day we are just extremely close friends."

Platonic, my ass. The man has had an erection for me more times than I can count. Not only does he openly eye-fuck me whenever I wear something tight or revealing, but has admitted dreaming about fucking me in ways that make me blush from just thinking about it.

Storm Ives has purposely got me hot and bothered, in need of sexual release and played with my hormones just for the mere fun of it and his sick satisfaction. Heck, we've even kissed with a passion threatening to burn us alive on the occasions we've slipped and briefly given in the sexual tension between us. Thankfully for both of our sakes, we've never, or rather, I've never let the two of us go any further than making out like two starving animals and blissful oral sex. I am a grown woman with need, after all.

"Yeah, platonic for sure," I mumbled loud enough for them to hear.

"Do you always walk around here with a gun on your hips?" Giving me an 'I don't believe you both' look, my father continued with his questioning.

"I don't, sir. And again, I apologise for pulling my weapon at you. But sir, I'll do it all over again if such a situation arises. My main aim and focus are to protect Angelica and Kyle and make sure nothing bad befalls on them." Squeezing his hand as a 'thank you', I was honestly appreciative of him.

In comparison to the people I've had in my life, Storm has always put me first, no matter what the situation, even when he gets mad at me. He is overprotective, yes, but I'm quite aware he only means good and wants what's best for me. His caring and loving self, among other aspects, are the main reason why I have stuck with him despite his playboy arrogant overconfident and often controlling demeanour.

Then again, my attitude and stubbornness have kicked his ass quite a few times, putting him back in place. This back and forth exchanges of power, our chemistry and the respect between us together with the ability to support each other's best and worst are what has been keeping our link strong. Especially when we get into testing each other's limits.

"Don't apologise for what's right, son. The knowledge that you would stop at nothing to protect our little girl and her kiddo is assurance enough for me to openly and heartily welcome you in my family."

"Thank you, sir. I highly appreciate it."

"You can drop the sir, Storm. The name is Auden, remember." Stretching his hand out to Storm, both men shook hands. The power in their handshake creating an unbreakable alliance between them.

"How close are you to Kyle, anyway?" My mom interrupted both men's bonding moment.

Unlike my dad, who had returned to his warm, loving self, my mom was still holding onto her iciness. Then again, anything less can't be expected from her.

"We are extremely close, ma'am. At first, Kyle had an understandable reserve towards me, but throughout the two-ish years I've been working with Angel, staying over here for days and babysitting him whenever Angel is absent or gone on a trip, Kyle and myself have grown really fond of each other. I teach and treat him like I would my own son if I had one."

Storm was soon going to make me teary if he doesn't stop. Gazing up at him, the desire to kiss him on the lips was driving me insane and causing butterflies to have a dancing party inside my stomach. His words and unusual spoken love for my son was making me wish I could tell my parents to fuck off somewhere else in the house while I straddle Storm and freely make-out with him.

"So you are not married, have a girlfriend or anything as such?"

Letting my mom's question sink in, I cracked up, "Girlfriend – and him?" Pointing at Storm, I let out a fit of laughter.

"As you can see, ma'am, I do not have any girlfriend or any sort of intimate long term relationship with anyone." Keeping his composure, Storm sent me an indisputable warning glare.

"Oh my God... That was funny..... Girlfriend, ha." Pushing aside his intense irrefutable reprimanding glare, I bellowed another fit of laughter.

"Are you done, Angelica?" My mom asked with a hint of impatience and curiosity. My dad, on the other hand, was on my side. He allowed himself to show his amusement through a smile.

"Mom, the man is a player." Chuckling, I voiced out a truth about Storm's character.

"A player, huh." Eyeing Storm with a scrutinising look that asked 'should I or should I not trust you? ', my mom glance between Storm and me once more.

"Allege player, ma'am. I'm mostly keeping to myself these days." Explaining himself, Storm tried to win a point with my mom. Little did he know it is close to impossible. Heck, even I am still trying to earn points with her, so who was he.

Enclosing his hand around mine in a firm redoubtable squeeze, Storm briefly imprisoned me in his greenish-greyish coloured eyes. Slightly gulping on my own spit, the message written in its depth was loud and clear as daylight. My impulsiveness to disobey his unmistakable forewarning to shut up and not to trigger him broke the well-locked box. A box whose dangerous contents were still vague to me.

To make matters worse, there was no way to lock it again. The deal was once I opened it, the contents of this box could be used against me at any time, and however much it was deemed necessary. It was definitive, I was now screwed until the end of days. Storm Ives was going to find a more than suitable punishment for me. Perceiving the evil glint in his eyes, the stupid and hormone-filled promises we made to each other a few months ago after a particularly sexual straining case clouded my mind.

#Flashback#

"What did you think of our case today?" Keeping his now empty container of food on his wooden table, Storm inquisitively inquired.

Finishing my food, I placed my empty container beside his and fully turned towards him with a perplexed look. "The BDSM murder case, you mean?"

"Yes." Shifting on his black wide leather couch, Storm answered with an almost nervous tone, confusing me.

"Other than how dangerous BDSM and their clubs can be, nothing much." Shrugging my shoulders, I didn't think twice about it.

"Technically Doc, neither the club nor the BDSM practices were at fault during this case. It was the apprentice member researching how to be a dominant who was at fault."

Observing his eyes darkened as he spoke of the BDSM club and its practices while running his eyes all over me, I finally understood his nervousness and the type of information he was trying to get out of me. Taking Storm by surprise, I slowly approached him with an evil smirk and climbed on top of his lap, my legs on either side of him.

"Doc." Storm warned, aware my intention was to tease him.

"Tell me, Stormie, did you get turned on watching all these submissives getting spanked, whipped, restraint, strapped and fuck like no tomorrow?" Bringing my lips inches away from his, eyes locked with each other, I sensually taunted.

"Doctor Buar!" Taking a deep sharp breath and closing his eyes, Storm attempted to regain control over himself. It was too late though, his manhood was already poking its interest at the subject at hand.

"That's my title, Detective Ives." Grasping his front shirt in my fist, I pulled hard, propelling his face and chest closer to me and his eyes to pop open.

"You are pushing it, Doc." His eyes pleading with me to reconsider my actions, or he won't be held responsible, I utterly disregarded his warning.

36

"What will you do, Detective? Will you punish me? – Will you cuff me, strap me down and whip me into submitting to what you consider good behaviour ….. Will you, Storm, bend me over this table behind me or on this couch under us? Will you spank my ass and eat me out to the point where I find it difficult to walk tomorrow morning?" Sexily and sultrily teasing Storm, I could see him breaking under my fingers.

Storm should have kept his mouth shut. This whole week was already filled with heightened sexual tension between us. This case and having to watch people torture and fuck each other into oblivion would do that to anyone. Now we were all alone in his apartment with completed paperwork on his living room table, and he had to open his beautifully shaped skilled lips and ask how I felt about the fucking case.

"FUCK!" Snapping under his breath, Storm took hold of the back of my neck and crashed his lips onto mine.

Kissing me like no tomorrow, he sharply pulled onto my hair and shoved his tongue inside my mouth without permission when it opened from the pain on my scalp. Hands flying everywhere, caressing my sides, my back, my hips, my thighs and my breasts, Storm devoured my lips.

"Why don't you listen when I ask you to stop?" Demanding in an almost pained tone, his breaths laboured, Storm kisses ran from my lips to my jawline to my neck as he ground me against his shaft.

"Maybe you should punish me, Detective." Continuously moving my hips on top of him, Storm bit down on the junction between my neck and my shoulder. Throwing my head back with a loud yelp, the realisation the game I was playing was verging on an extremely dangerous point dawned on me.

"Maybe I should."

Left with no time to think about his words or what was happening, Storm pushed me off him and flipped me onto the couch with my ass up in the air in a flash. Shoving my office skirt over my ass and on top of my hips before I could utter a word, Storm literally ripped my lacy blue panties off me like a brute.

"Storm! – What are you doing?" Feeling fear and anticipation for what's to come pulsing through me, I was confused if I should scream at Storm out of pleasure and lust or anger and fear.

"Why, punishing you of course." Skimming his hand over my butt cheeks a couple of times, his eyes practically burning holes on my ass, Storm declared as if he was announcing the most natural and normal thing in the universe.

"Storm, you are not a dominant. You just watched them and took a few introductory classes as did I."

"Actually Doc, that's not true. I lied to you when I said I didn't know anything about the BDSM world. I wanted to see your reaction to that side of the world."

Confused and slightly turned on from his skimming hand on my buttocks, "What?"

"Did you seriously think getting into such a private and prestigious club as easily as we did was normal?"

"No – but..."

"Doc, I have been a dominant and a member of that particular club for years now. It has branches all over the country, and the owner is a good friend of mine. You, Doc, were introduced as my submissive behind closed doors. One who was new and unaware of the BDSM world. Reasons why we took the classes. And I gotta tell you, Angel, watching you get aroused and smelling the arousal off you while you were studying them was a major turned on. – Trust me when I tell you; being a submissive is what you need deep down."

Astounded at the normality of his voice, I found it hard to retaliate. Sliding his hands and emitting extreme warmth down my inner thighs, Storm spread my legs further apart without any warning. He was lucky I was already holding onto the armrest of the couch for dear life. The fear within me only increasing with every passing second of his caress on my ass.

I didn't fear Storm, per se, I trusted the man with mine and my kid's life. What I was dreading was what we were doing. I was afraid we will go too far and not be able to return back like the usual. Moreover, I watched those submissives for hours and days on end, I wasn't sure I was ready to play in the court they did.

Gliding his fingers on my slick and throbbing womanhood, I tensed up when Storm applied pressure on my entrance from the back. "Storm, wait!" Turning my head towards him and maintaining position, "I don't think I can do this. Sorry."

Slowly leaning forward, his face dangerously close to mine, Storm fisted the back of my hair. Pulling my face upward, his hot breaths were doing tricks inside my body.

"What did I say you should have done, Angel?" With a hint of danger in his tone, Storm demanded.

"To stop." Looking straight into his eyes, I answered in a low tone.

"Did I or did I not give you fair warning of what was going to happen if you didn't stop?" Without mercy, Storm questioned with authoritativeness. His bulging length pressed against my bare ass, as unforgiving as him.

"You did, and I'm sorry. I promise to not go this far next time."

"Babe, you don't get to tease me as such with the clear intention of leaving me hanging and not pay the price for it."

"Please Storm. I know I'm sexually frustrating you to the point of no return and I'll make up for it. But this BDSM stuff right now would bring things too far, and I'm afraid I won't be able to hold back as usual." Finding no reason to hide my true feelings and thoughts from him, I blurb out the truth.

"Why do you insist on holding back? We can be good together." Touching his forehead to mine, Storm asked in a much gentler tone.

"I'm sorry Storm, but you know how I feel about relationships and commitment. I simply can't put myself through all of what it means and brings with it."

"You realise I will never truly intentionally hurt you or your heart. Punishment through BDSM is utterly different from intentional physical abuse. You've been with me throughout this whole case to know it is a form of love, lust, discipline, respect, power and release of any sort. Heck, it is even therapeutic for some."

Supporting my weight on only one arm, I grabbed the back of Storm's neck with my other hand and press his forehead further into mine. "This is why I am so apologetic about it. Truthfully part of me wants this; wants us. Even the punishment you were going to inflict on me, but a major part of me knows there is a limit we cannot cross just yet."

Releasing a breath, "Fine. If you don't want to do this right now, we won't. But on only one condition."

Fixing my eyes on his with curiosity and slight trepidation, "What?" I simply mumbled.

"I'll postpone the punishing until next time you push my buttons despite my warnings. It can be for sexual or non-sexual reasons. And because I'm being so lenient and considerate towards you right now, I'm now allowed to punish you in any way I deem fit every single time I feel I'm being purposely disobey or just for my mere pleasure once this box is cracked open. Think carefully over what it all means, before you answer, Doc." With finality in his tone, I realised I had only two choices.

Take his offer for later when I'm more under control and unlikely to misbehave as much or get punished right now where I will most definitely lose control.

"Deal. I accept your conditions."

"Great. Good girl." Patting me on my hair, Storm retreated back.

"Hold onto the couch armrest for me."

"What? – Why?" Perplexed, I instantly enjoined, the uncertainty of this moment not sitting well with me.

"Our promises was about me not punishing you right now, not about refraining myself from having a taste of you. Now, don't make me repeat myself, grab the armrest." Nudging my legs apart with his knee this time, I watched Storm dived between my legs.

5

"**A**ngel, – Angelica Buar!" Hearing my full name, I pulled myself back to the present world where Storm was not making me scream to high hell but quietly sitting beside me with a mischievous knowing smirk and glimmer.

"Sorry, you were saying?" I asked my mom.

"Well, I was originally asking why you never mentioned Detective Storm to us or us to him, but now I want to know where you got lost at?"

"Oh, I wanna know too? – It's not every day I get to see my daughter's face turn this shade of pink." My father added with amusement and excitement.

Feeling more colours rush to my face, "I've mentioned you two to Storm more times than I can count, I just haven't shown him any pictures. However, I've never mentioned Detective Storm to you guys because we rarely ever speak. We've skype less than ten times in the past five years. Do you seriously think I would spend my time talking about my friends, much less my friendship with Storm? A friendship which brings a whole lot of attention and questions on its own. I know you and dad too much; you would have pestered me about Storm every single time, demanding why I'm not in a serious romantic relationship with the guy."

"And can you blame us. You gotta admit, the friendship - as you put it- between you two is odd and peculiar." Aware I didn't hold any grudge against the two of them since this was just how our situation was, my mom, shook off my comment about our limited communication.

After sending my ex-husband, Dylan Henry, to jail for continuous domestic abuse despite his promises to never lay a hand on me, I ran away, seven months pregnant with Kyle. Apparently, I had ruin Dylan's life by stupidly getting myself pregnant, when it was he who didn't care to wear protection while forcing himself onto me. The man was sick. He loved and enjoyed taking me by force with no consideration of where we were. As per his philosophy, he owned me and had the right to do whatever the fuck he wanted with me just because we were married.

The day my doctor informed me I was going to lose my child if I didn't stop having rough sex while being so heavily pregnant – as if I had a choice in the latter- was the day all hell broke loose. Giving birth to my little angel was the only thing I was truly living for back then, and the news had devastated me. I had known then I had no other choice but to step it up and be my own woman.

Taking the help of my parents while I was still with Dylan was a big no-no. Not only had Dylan threatened to physically hurt them if I ever opened my mouth to utter a word against him, but he also had them wrapped around his fingers. The man was the reincarnation of the devil himself. He was slick, cunning, Machiavellian, devious and expertly knew how to play people.

Standing up for myself for the first time after being crushed under Dylan's thumb for so long was the best thing I could have done for myself. Returning home that night after speaking with the doctor about everything I would need to make sure my baby survives, I turned on the recording on my phone, increased the sensitivity to its highest and stuffed it inside my pocket. Marching into the living room where Dylan was lounging on the couch, chugging his third bottle of beer, I took a deep, courageous breath, hoping my plan would work or I was beyond screwed.

To this very day, I still feel dread coursing through me and shudder at the memory of Dylan's devilish smirk and menacing shimmer glazing in his eyes whenever he readied himself to pounce on me or force me to do something I didn't want to.

Explaining the baby situation to Dylan and confronting him that night, I refused to give him a blowjob for the very first time, despite knowing he would push me to the edge to get what he wants, whether I accept or not. Fisting my hair, nearly ripping it off my scalp, Dylan violently threw me down.

Wrapping my arms around my belly in an attempt to protect my baby and my stomach, I fell face first on the flooring. Pleading Dylan to stop and just let me be, his eyes flashed with pleasure. My screams to cease his torment, giving him a bigger boner. Watching with horror as Dylan unzipped and stepped out of his pants, my need to escape heightened, but my resolution to act had taken a toll from the fall. Menacingly marching towards me, the thudding of his every step resounded like impending doom and death.

Raising my head up by my hair, Dylan took his hardening dick in his other hand and pressed it against my lips. Slapping me hard across my face a couple of times at my unwillingness to cooperate, Dylan got exasperated and took my jaw in his hand. Crying at the non-consensual abuse on my face, it became effortless for Dylan to force my lips open and shove his dick inside my mouth.

His biggest mistake and foremost reason for his downfall, however, was him threatening to kick the life out of my unborn baby while it was still in my stomach if I didn't cooperate. Especially since the biggest issue for him not being able to fuck me as roughly and hard as he desired was the concern I had for the safety of the child. Pressing his length deeper and relentlessly fucking my mouth, a wave of courage and strength washed over me, and I bit down on his manhood. Screeching in pain, he immediately backed away from me.

Rising to my feet, I kicked him on the calf and sped out of the apartment as fast as my seven months pregnant self could. Not stopping until I was inside the nearest police station with the recording as proof and leverage for my protection, I regain my freedom that same night.

Afterwards, I realized there wasn't anything left except suffocation and fear for me in that State. Grabbing the bare minimal the next day, I ran away without informing anyone, preparing myself for a new life as a single mother. Thankfully I had always had a passion for Cognitive psychology and had my master on it.

Willing myself to practice in this field, which I had come to believe was not for me due to Dylan's constant statements of my incapability on the subject, and how I was not made for it, I took an internship with the first company that showed interest in me. I worked my butt off and viciously proved Dylan wrong. Proved myself I was worth something. In less than five years, I managed to become the well-known doctor I am today and got one of the most prominent positions at a prestige university dedicated to medicine and science.

"You alright, Doc?" Gently squeezing my hand, Storm asked with a genuine concern for my well being.

Back to the present, I shook off the hurt from the distasteful memory of Dylan Henry. Stretching my lips into a bright but fake smile, "Sorry. I'm good – Just Dylan." Gazing up to Storm, I mumbled.

As perceptive as Storm was, he looked right past my fake-ass reassuring smile within a split second. "We are done with the questioning!" Rising up to his feet and pulling me up with him, Storm declared with a finality not meant to be challenged.

"Excuse me?" Standing up as well, my mom posed with a raised eyebrow, defying Storm on the point.

"Ma'am, Auden, I am once again sorry but will all due respect, I refuse to put Angelica through the torturous memory of her ex-husband."

"Storm, it's fine." In a low voice that indicated it clearly wasn't just fine, I attempted to appease Storm.

"No, it is not Ang. We both know the pattern like no other. You think of the asshole, get engulfed in the past with him and have horrible vivid nightmares for nights. You are strong, and I really don't know how you do it, but there's only so much I can take. Having to calm you down and watch you fight me until you fully come back to the present is painful for me." Giving him a grateful but small smile, I wasn't even mad he was divulging way too much of our private moments.

Turning his attention back to my parents, "I figured you two are perplexed, inquisitive and even concern about Angel and her relationship with me, but know I only have her best interest at heart. Yes, our relationship is out-of-norms, confusing, complex and even weird to most. But the only thing that should matter to you guys is I care for Angelica and would readily give my life for her. If that's all for now, please excuse us, I have a surprise waiting for Angel."

"A surprise?" Pushing aside the warmth trying to drown my heart and the powerful hammering his words and actions were inflicting against the wall securing my heart from falling in love with the man, I concentrated on the surprise aspect of his statement.

"Yes, Doc, a surprise." Beaming down at me, Storm picked my interest furthermore. Certainly, he couldn't mean the punishment awaiting me at the end of tonight. Not in front of my parents.

"What is it?" Quizzically eyeballing Storm, I probed.

As if reading my mind, Storm slid his arm around the back of my waist and gave it a discreet squeeze.

"A little something me and Kyle concocted and hid last night."

Swiftly looking between him and Kyle, I was more than intrigued.

"You guys are more than welcome to follow us. I might be over-protective of Angelica, but I mean no disrespect. You both are always welcome to be part of whatever it is we do as a family." Regarding my parents with respect and an apologetic gleam for snapping at them, Storm invited them open-heartedly.

"You two go ahead, Elize and I would shortly join you. We need to have a brief private discussion."

"As you wish, Auden." Nodding his head at Storm in response, my father remained silent and waited for us to walk out of the living room.

Gibbing at Storm, "So… you care for me, huh? – Have the best interest for me at heart, are over-protective of me and would readily give your life for me. – And what else, huh, Storm? … Are you also going to say I'm the love of your life?"

Abruptly stopping us on our way to the kitchen, Storm gawked at me, his eyes flashing to a darker green. "I would highly advise against jeering about such matter, Doc. You are already on a short leash!" Warning me, Storm continued to lead me to the kitchen.

"But what if I say I'm soaked from everything you've done and said since you've stepped foot in here tonight?"

What the actual fuck was wrong with me? I knew I was already in trouble with him, so why was I continuously tempting my chance? Where did my ability to shut it fly to?

Hearing Storm intake a deep harsh breath to keep himself sane, my heart flutter at the knowledge of how vulnerable such a big man like him was to my mere words. Directing me behind the kitchen counter, Storm brusquely dragged my body into his.

Crashing into his firm muscular self, towering me with no problem, "Storm! – My parents can walk in on us at any moment."

Glancing at the kitchen threshold, with the living room's opening only a few feet away, a rush of excitement and nervousness coursed through me.

"I keep warning you to behave, but all you keep doing is misbehave and tease the fuck out of me." Storm stated in a strained tone. Directing my chin up and captivating my gaze, the tribulation awaiting me was crystal clear.

"I'm sorry. I just can't seem to stop myself from teasing you. Your expression and reaction are too priceless."

"You know whose expression and reaction are going to be priceless tonight?" Sliding his hand from my back down to my buttocks, Storm slapped my assets, causing me to intake a sharp breath.

"Storm, my parents!" My eyes pleaded with him for more, contradicting my resistance and words.

Clasping my butt with pressure, "You're parents are not going to be an excuse tonight. You are going to be punished and not as gingerly as I had originally planned, Doc."

Pushing my front into him, his length grazed against my sweatpants. With my lacy thong soaked beyond belief by now, it became more of a pleasure inflicting material as it increased the pressure between my legs when Storm pressed himself against me.

Capturing my lips with his for a millisecond, making me purr like a cat, "Prepare that ass for me, babe. I'm gonna teach you some much-needed manners."

Huskily taunting me, Storm dropped his hands from my body and put some distance between us, giving me a taste of my own medicine. Glowering at him with disbelief, I got to feel the sexual frustration he must feel when I get him going just like he did me and back away when the tension and desire rise to a suffocating degree. And I must admit, it isn't really a great feeling.

I wanted to choke the life out of Storm for making me feel this way. Watching his smirk, I realized my punishment was not going to start later on tonight. – It had already begun.

6

"So, where is this aforementioned surprise?" Breaking Storm and my electrical gaze, my mom astonished both of us. Standing in front of the kitchen counter, my dad and mom expectedly waited with a knowing look.

Blushing a darker shade of pink at the possibility of them witnessing whatever went on between Storm and myself in the limited amount of time we were left alone, I successfully kept my mouth shut.

"I still have to show her. Doc and I were having an extremely important discussion." Taking charge, and acting absolutely unfazed, as if nothing happened between us moments ago and he didn't just have another boner, Storm clarified for my parents.

"Go ahead, then. Unless you guys need more private time to discuss?" Quirking his eyebrow at us, my father's comment was laced with suggestiveness.

"No! We are fine. We don't need any more private time – to discuss." I announced way too quickly for it to not sound suspicious.

Sniggering under his breath, Storm made his way to my refrigerator. Disregarding my desire to smack his laugh away, I instead followed the movement of his well-built arms; feeling like his dress shirt was going to give out and rip from muscular flexing.

"Herb seasoned chicken?" Confused like no tomorrow, I stared at the bowl of uncooked cold chicken meat seasoned with herbs, garlic, lime and black pepper Storm had placed in front of me.

"You want me to cook for you or something?" Looking up at Storm, I voiced out my puzzlement.

Laughing at me again, Storm tousled my hair, "No, Ang. I'm going to be the one cooking for you. I learned this new plate when you were gone and thought it would be a great surprise for when you return. – What do you think?"

Looking at me expectedly, with excitement glimmering in the depth of his eyes, I leaned into Storm and plaster a gentle kiss on his cheek. "I love the surprise."

Putting his arm around my opposite shoulder, Storm gave me a side hug. "I'm glad you did. I almost thought you would think it was a stupid idea and surprise."

"Never." Smiling up at Storm, I quickly reassured the big man. His gentle acts, no matter how cheesy was always welcome and appreciated.

Ahem *Ahem* *Ahem*

Loudly clearing his throat, my father promptly separated us. Jumping out of Storm's embrace as if I had gotten burned, I felt like a teenager being caught doing something terrible. Avoiding my parents' gazes and returning my heartbeat to normal, I mumbled a string of curses under my breath.

"Did you say something, Angel?" My mom quipped with a sly smirk.

"Hum… just asking Storm if he needed help." I quickly saved myself from more embarrassment.

"I'm good, Doc. If I have you cook with me, the whole concept of me cooking for you as a surprise would be ruined."

"Don't be stupid. I'm gonna help you with dinner."

Stubborn, I stood my ground. Not because I was a big lover of cooking but because it was an excellent evasion tactic. If I cook, I don't have to undergo another interrogation and be subject to piercing soul searching eyes.

"No, you are not." Storm refused to let me ruin his surprise.

Staring and challenging each other, it dawned on me that only a compromise would work. "How about I help you out with the prepping, and you do all the cooking? Like this, you maintain your surprise."

Looking at me and contemplating my idea, "Fine. I'll go get you a glass of your favourite wine then. Start cutting the vegetables and onions I put aside into cubes." Storm finally agreed.

Leaving me alone with my parents, the asshole knew precisely why I had volunteered to help him and found a perfect excuse to leave me alone with my parents.

"You're sure you two are not more than friends? The electricity between you two can power a whole village." My dad incredulously posed.

'The electricity might be coming from my strong desire to murder his ass right now.' I mentally stated.

"Yes, dad. I'm certain." Peeling the onion and running it under hot water, I robotically answered.

"Have you two dated before being just friends?" My mom asked this time around.

"You two are reading too much into us. We. are. Just. friends." Not meeting their eyes head-on because God knows we are more than just platonic friends, I expressed my point.

"Are you interested in dating the man?" Brushing my explicit words, my father inquired.

"Dad! We work together, and we are just -"

"Friends." My mom sing-sang.

"Exactly."

"That still doesn't answer my question." Pestering me and refusing to drop the subject, my father wasn't doing any favour to the wall trying to rebuild itself around my heart.

"Dad, how about you go help Storm with that wine? I feel like I'm going to need the entire bottle."

Shooing my father away, I left it to Storm to deal with him. Besides, it was payback for leaving me alone with them. Especially when I haven't lived with those people for over seven years now.

"Are you going to push me away too?" Steepling her fingers together, her chin resting on the back of her hand, my mom flatly spelt out.

"No, mother. Not unless you keep hounding me with questions about Storm and me. Especially when I'm tearing up from trying to cut this damn onion." Letting her on how I felt about this whole situation, I gave her a choice.

~~ | | ~~

~ *Storm's P.O.V*~

Intrigued by the sudden unannounced arrival of Angel's parents at her place, I couldn't help but wonder what could have triggered such a turn in events. Last I heard they were back home in New Hampshire living with her millionaire brother and barely making an effort to stay in consistent contact with Angel. Nevertheless, I understood that I would have to wait until tonight to interrogate Angel to know what's actually happening.

Oh, tonight... Just thinking about it is making my pant shift and the space within diminishing. Angelica had nowhere to escape tonight. My soul and body wanted to be one with Angel. To dive my entire self into her delicacy; to feel her wall closing around my throbbing length as I make her come for me alone.

Then again, I recognized I would have to wait far longer before this dream of mine could come true. And as much as it kills and hurt me, I respected Angel's decision. Understood her pain and how she was still healing. The necessity to stand on her own two feet and be a success for her son and herself was beyond essential for her.

Nonetheless, I see tonight as a significant step forward. Tonight, Doctor Angelica Buar was going to vanquish her fear of BDSM. She knew the conditions and broke open the box. Her punishment was definite and inevitable.

I, on the other hand, would most certainly have to fuck one of my previous dates by tomorrow night to get rid of the tension that's only going to increase throughout the night. But the joy of smacking Angel's firm perfectly round shape ass and teaching her how to behave more appropriately would be worth it.

The woman was an exceptional tease; my own personal torturer and most definitely the death of me. The cases of blue balls I've gained from her alone was remarkably immense and unbelievable. Then she wonders why I'm such a player. She is the fucking damn reason.

"Woh, son! ... Look where you are going." Two hands landing on my shoulder blades, I was forced to stop on my way back from checking up on Kyle.

My attention was drawn back to the present, "Sorry, Auden. My mind was elsewhere." Staring at the man, I sincerely apologized.

"Clearly. You nearly knocked me over." Jesting, Auden gave me a small man pat on the shoulder.

"I'll take a wild guess and say Doc kicked you out of the kitchen." Cocking my eyebrow at Auden, we stood side by side, between the living room and kitchen threshold. Away from the women's earshot.

"Nah. I was just sent out on a mission to hunt down tonight's chef. But most importantly, to recoup my daughter's nectar of the night."

Directing my gaze to the wine bottle in my hand, "This, you mean." Smiling at the old man, I let him have this win. Angel had totally kicked him out of the kitchen for asking way too many questions.

"Here, let me take it."

"Sure, why not." Handing him the bottle, I began to make my way to the glass cabinet.

"Detective Ives, what's your intention towards my daughter?"

I knew this was coming. – I just fucking knew it.

Slowly returning my gaze on the man, "What do you mean, Auden? I believe I have already been clear about my intention." Dismissing the seriousness dancing in the depth of Auden's eyes, I stood my ground.

"My daughter can't hear us, Storm, so let's have a real man to man conversation. I might have been an absent father in her life, but I am not stupid. I've closely observed the look and glint in your eyes every single time you look at my daughter."

"I don't know what you are speaking of, Auden? Like I mentioned earlier, our relationship is platonic. Nothing is going on."

Deny. Deny. Deny. I executed my main plan and my only possible way out.

"Your words, actions, posture and expression cannot be denied, Storm. Nor can the erection you've gotten at least twice since you've stepped foot in here tonight."

Shocked, embarrassed and out of words to deny, I gulped down on my own spit. 'I have a feeling I'm going to need that bottle of wine as much as Angel, tonight.' Dancing my eyes between Auden, Angelica behind the kitchen counter and the far-away exit door, I was trapped.

"That's what I thought. – Now, if you are done bullshitting me, do you want to try again? … What's your intention and expectation out of my daughter?"

Determined and stubborn, just like Angelica, Auden successfully intimidated me. As they say, never come between a father and his little princess.

Locking our gazes briefly, I inhaled a courageous breath and stared at the woman behind the counter chopping vegetables. "If you are asking if we are having sexual intercourse, sir, the answer is no. My intention and expectation from Angelica are exception-ally pure. I care for her and her kid. The woman is, so God damn strong, courageous, caring, smart, gorgeous, sassy, determined and stubborn, it is hard to not fall in love with her."

Returning my full attention back on Auden, I held him a prison-er of my serious gaze. "If I had my way, Auden, your daughter would have long been my girlfriend. I would probably be meeting up with you right now to ask her hand in marriage; not having the discussion we currently are. But that's not the case. – Angelica has her own baggage she is too scared to fully unpack yet, and I respect her decision because I love her. All I know is there's going to come a time where she will be my wife."

Silently listening without judgement, Auden nodded in under-standing. "Have you at least try telling her how you really feel?"

"She knows I like her and wants nothing more but to date her. Heck, I even promised her I would drop my player habits in a heartbeat if she said yes."

His interest more than picked, "What did she say?"

"She appreciated my complete honesty and wished she could say yes. Part of her wants us to happen and be a reality as much as I do. But she is still driven by her fear and is not going to let go anytime soon. – It is fine, though. I have waited for a few years already, so what's another year."

Placing his hand on my right shoulder, Auden firmly applied pressure. "I'm sorry about your predicament, son. I wish I could do something to help the two of you become one."

Sending Auden a reassuring smile, "It's okay, Auden. I appreciate your desire to help. If Angelica and I are destined to be together, we will be at the end. Until then, I'll be what she needs me to be, along with being the father figure Kyle sees in me. Plus I get to hold onto my title as a player. – You got no idea how frustrating Angel can be when she wants to."

"If your earlier erections in front of her own parents were any indication, I would say a whole lot." With a sly smirk and a highly suggestive tone, Auden used his new found weapon against me.

OUCH!

7

Observing and studying the deep intense conversation between Storm and my dad, I had the sudden desire to be a fly on the wall behind them. Fiercely cutting the vegetable Storm had kept on the counter, I was having a bad feeling.

I shouldn't have left my dad and Storm alone. God only knows what nonsense they were talking about. But whatever it was, I knew I was involved. Storm's posture and searching eyes were indicative of that much.

Oh my gosh, what if Storm lets our unconventional relationship slip? Tell the truth about our partly sexual life?

OUCH!

Slicing the razor sharp knife through my forefinger, I screamed out in pain. What the fuck was I thinking, blindly cutting things into small pieces?

Not giving me time to bash at myself, Storm was already by my side within seconds, holding my hand up and glaring down at me. Behind his furious glare, however, I could discern the panic and worry.

"What the fuck is wrong with you, Ang! – Using a sharp object with divided attention! … I can't even leave you alone for five minutes! What were you thinking?"

"You're ranting, babe. I'm fine. It's just a small cut." Resting my uninjured hand on top of Storm's shoulder in an attempt to ease his mind and reduce his scolding, I momentarily forgot about my own pain and the blood gushing out of my finger.

"Unless small cuts produce this amount of blood, Doc, I don't think it's fine. Now, go sit on that stool. I need to take a better look at it."

"Storm, you're worrying too much. It's a cut, it will heal in no time." Giving Storm attitude, his combination of caring, concern, frustration and anger was conflicting with my pain and my attempt to reassure and calm him down.

"Doctor Angelica Buar, you either willingly sit your ass on that stool, or I'll sit you down there myself!"

Fiercely glaring at me, I recognized I was in deep shit. The manner and tone Storm used while uttering my full name was more than enough indication. He wouldn't hesitate to manhandle me in front of my parents if my health was at stake.

"Do you want me to address you as Master next?"

Then again, nobody said I was the brightest crayon in the box. Tempting, arguing and bluntly disobeying a man who takes his role as a dominant seriously has to be one of the worst decisions I've made so far. The pleasure and fun from it all, though were worth it.

"Last warning, Angelica!"

"Fine." Discerning the ultimatum and danger as he spelt out each word, I stomped my feet and sat my behind on the stool as ordered.

I wasn't pleased. Taking orders from a man wasn't something I did any longer, but I soon realized that at the end of the day, Storm immensely cared for me. He wanted nothing but the best for me. Furthermore, I was already getting punished tonight, I didn't need to add more pain to my future punishment.

Detaching the first aid kit from under the kitchen counter, Storm pulled out a square disinfecting wipe, the smell of the alcohol as strong as ever. Taking my bloody finger in his hand, Storm began to clean the blood. Starting from the unlashed part.

"Ow!" Yelping and cringing, I nearly jumped out of my seat the instant the alcoholic pad grazed the gash. Feeling fire running through my arm, I looked up at Storm; unsure if I should glare at him with anger or pain.

"Sorry," Apologetic and further concerned, Storm kept his voice low.

"You better be! This shit flares up like fire on my finger." Snapping, my body had already decided which emotion to concentrate on.

Wordless, Storm grabbed my other hand and placed it on top of his chest. "Pay close attention to my heartbeat and don't take your eyes off mine no matter what. I might need to do a minor stitch for quicker healing."

"You're serious." Bewildered, I searched his eyes.

"Very."

Yep, the man was not joking. Nodding my head at Storm, I braced myself against the fiery sting and future stabbing of needles. Locked in his gaze, his heart beating at a fair pace in comparison to mine, I obliged myself to limit my hissing and not let my gaze drop from him or trail to my fingers.

Losing myself, I admired Storm's features, his long nose; the way he squinted his beautiful greenish almond eyes and the grey outlining his iris when he was concentrating. The corner of his wide lips twitching every so often, mainly when I would instinctively hiss made me wish I could run my tongue over the natural line of his mouth. I wanted to bite down on the teardrop of his lips and flick my tongue over his cupid bow.

Enjoying this unique time to truly break down each and every section of Storm's face, his jawline, his square cheekbone, his neck, his forehead, his hair and even his general size ears, the beauty of Storm Ives hugely increased in my eyes. His concern and the gentleness he was using could be read on his face like an open book. Feeling his heart race under my fingertips, I realized my intense close studying of his features was greatly influencing him. He could feel my eyes caressing his soft skin.

"You are doing great, Ang. Just a few more minutes."

Breaking my ferocious ogling to a mere stare, I sensed him bandaging a sterile pad on my finger. I couldn't believe Storm had managed to take my pain away without me even realizing it.

"Storm, what happened to mommy?" Hearing Kyle's voice from a distance, I wanted to turn to him but somehow couldn't bring

57

myself to avert my eyes from Storm.

"Mommy learned why playing with sharp objects while being distracted is bad." In a scolding and preaching tone, Storm proclaimed. His seriousness top notched.

"Now stay put. I'll go get you your drink." Capturing my gaze with his imperious one, Storm ordered me around again.

Seriously, why was I letting the man make demands and commands? After Dylan, I had sworn to never ever let anyone, much less a man ordain me around. As if I was there property. So what the actual fuck was happening here? Why was Storm's domineering side not scaring me or making me severely angry? Why was I liking the combination of sweet, caring, forgiving, loving, commanding, dominating and bossiness in Storm Ives? What was wrong with me!?

"But mommy is all fine now, don't worry." My mom added.

Hearing her voice, brusquely brought me to the reality that my parents were here the whole freaking time. They saw me stupidly following Storm's instruction, me openly ogling him with desire-filled eyes and worst, heard me address Storm as, babe. Profusely blushing, I slowly turned my body towards my mom, dad and Kyle.

"Oh, hi, mom, dad." Embarrassing myself, even more, the redness on my face considerably increased.

"Hi, daughter. How's that finger?" Jesting, my dad quirked his eyebrow at me. The old man knew something; the glint in his eyes told me as much.

Could I possibly use Storm's interrogation office and probe my father into answering all my questions.

"Angel, your drink." Placing the glass, filled up to the brick, in front of me, Storm pulled me out of my master plan to get the truth out of my father.

"Thanks, Storm. For the drink and taking care of this." Lifting my bandaged fingers, I fully showed him my appreciation. The bitchiness and attitude from earlier vanished into thin air.

"You're welcome, Doc." Smiling down at me, I knew all was forgiven. Storm was simply worried to death about me.

"Mommy, Storm, I'm starving." Standing in front of my mother's legs, Kyle voiced out. It was, after all, nearing dinner time.

"No worries, bud. I'm making dinner tonight. It will be ready in a few. How about you sit with mommy and watch me cook? Like this, you can cook for mommy next time she hurts herself." Excitedly nodding at Storm, Kyle took his seat beside me, eagerly waiting to learn. I swear Storm has a magical way with kids.

"So Storm, tell me, where did you learn how to stitch so professionally?" Taking her seat on the other stool beside me, with my father by her side, my mom inquired. At least now she was taking a real interest in the man as a person instead of merely concentrating on his relationship with me.

"I started my career in the army, ma'am. After several years overseas, I transferred to the Marshall in the States and moved to having my own team of Detectives with the State Law Enforcement after working my first case with your daughter." Busying himself with frying, Storm answered. His ability to multi-task with such efficiency and flow fascinating me as usual.

"One case with Angelica and you moved down to Detective? That's peculiar." My dad commented, interested to know the back story.

The look he and Storm momentarily shared right after those words left his mouth, however, spoke volumes. Both men definitely had something going on between them.

"Not peculiar, Auden, just interesting. Angel's and my first case was purely accidental. She had just gotten recognized for the best Cognitive behavioural psychologist, profiler and analyst when we first met. I was tasked to apprehend an individual for a crime I can't divulge, and there was Doctor Angelica Buar, speaking with my suspect -"

"A suspect whom I told you was innocent, but you simply couldn't care less. You were all *'I don't care what you say. If you want to prove him non-guilty, then go ahead, you have a free pass.'* But guess who was right, huh?" Announcing the victory of my first case, the pride I felt back then still coursed through me. The end of that case was a life-changer; a blessing in disguise.

"A free pass which I got in trouble for. The havoc Miss Buar, here, caused to have her point heard while announcing her free pass to the world is the reason we are where we are today. Long story short, Auden, my boss was immensely impressed by the Doctor's work and our chemistry that he created a whole investigative branch with a few of our other friends and colleagues. Becoming the lead Detective was my punishment for giving Angel a free pass to solve a crime she wasn't even supposed to be involved in."

"So if you two didn't run into each other that day, we all wouldn't be here right now, being dished up by you?" My mom stated more than asked.

Nodding, we all walked to the dining table, more than ready to devour the well-presented food Storm had prepared. The fantastic smell rising from the plate itself was making my stomach growled and my mouth water.

8

"Kyle, time for bed, baby." Calling for Kyle when the clock hit eight, I tried to get his attention away from his game.

After our delicious filling dinner, Kyle had brushed and gone back to the TV to finish his racing game. While us adults went to the couch for another prolonged conversation. One far less intimidating and exhausting than the first one.

Clearing the flooring, Kyle kept his game back, jumpily made his way to me and sat on my lap with an innocent look. Smiling down at him, I secured him in my arms as he cuddled up on me and his face pillowed on my shoulder. Cradling him, I waited until his entire body was fully relaxed and walked us to his bedroom. Gently laying my little angel down in his car shape bed, I tucked him in and took a seat beside his bed.

"Which story would you like today, bud?" Dimming the light behind him, Storm softly asked while going through Kyle's little library of kids books.

"Would you continue the pig and wolf story, please?" With excited eyes and a small yawn, Kyle requested.

"Do you remember where we stopped the last time?" Sitting across from me, Strom flipped through the pages as quietly as possible.

"The big bad wolf blew off the first pig's hay house." His attention entirely on Storm, Kyle small hand held tight onto mine.

This was his little gesture to let me know he wanted both me and

Storm here with him. Bringing the back of his little hand to my lips, I laid a gentle yet firm kiss, letting him know I loved being here too.

Clearing his throat, the storyteller in Storm captivated both mine and Kyle's utter attention. I was so engrossed in this fatherly side of Storm, I barely noticed when Kyle's hold on my hand loosen, and he fell asleep. Much less the presence of my parents at the door and their silent studious searching eyes.

Placing a light kiss on Kyle's forehead after Storm, I neatly rested his hand on top of his chest and whispered my unconditional love for him. Silently and stealthily walking out, we let the door crack about two fingers from the frame - just the way Kyle likes it.

"Kyle likes and expect Storm to read him a story every time he stays this late or overnight. Usually, it is me, or Ana if I'm late. You guys are welcome to volunteer to read him his bedtime stories and see if he lets you." I basically blabbered the instant we all walked back to the living room. Their questions were inevitable, so why not tackle it beforehand.

"Thanks for the clarification, Angelica." Musing, my mom tried to hold back her chuckle.

Surprisingly after me stupidly cutting my finger; Storm heroically taking care of it, and her having an eerie private conversation with my dad, my mom became more easy-going. It was like she was finally letting loose and had actually taken an extreme liking of Storm. I wasn't sure what the actual deal was; I was just glad my mom was enjoying herself to the point of making jokes.

"Are you staying late or over tonight, Storm?" Peculiarly raising his eyebrow at Storm then at me and back to Storm, my dad made me nervous. I felt like I was back in high school and asking my dad if I could have my boyfriend stay the night and promising we will keep our hands to ourselves.

"Staying the night, Auden. Angel and I have a case to work on." Storm announced way too casually.

"At this hour of the night?" Perplexed, my mom questioned.

"Crime doesn't wait on anyone, nor does it look at the time, ma'am."

"Is that so?" Arching a brow, Storm's hook line seemed to have captured her interest.

"He's exaggerating, mom. We've been working the same case for over a week now. I need to catch up with the progress he and our team made while I was in New Hampshire for a speech on my previous Neuron-link research."

"We also need to work on new avenues and strategies before Monday, or the commissioner will have my head." Slicing his hand over his neck, Storm almost cracked me up. He was such a goofball sometimes.

"Don't worry about your pretty head. I'm here now, and will not sleep until we have a glimpse of a possible breakthrough." Standing on my tiptoes, I messed with Storm's mass of styled jet black hair.

"Thank God for the Doctor and her smarts." Smirking, Storm had me roll my eyes at him.

"You kids have fun then. We will be heading to bed." Smiling at us, my dad took my mom's hand into his. His simple action causing my own hand to itch in need to reach out for Storm's hands. Thankfully, I promptly stopped myself and my childish desire.

Yawning, "Sleep sounds wonderful after that long flight. My back is starting to screech its complaint at me." Gently rubbing her lower back, my mom seemed more than ready to crash.

"Mom, you should stop forcing your back. When it hurts, you stop and take a break." Scolding her like a child, I almost laughed at the reverse in roles. The daughter had become the mother.

"Yes, mother." Literally rolling her eyes at me; the mother became the child in a snap.

Shaking my head at my mom's sassiness and sarcasm; which I have clearly gotten from her, I walked up to them. "Goodnight, mom." Kissing her on the cheek, I slightly took her by surprise.

I had almost forgotten kissing goodnight was a tradition only maintained in my house here, not in my entire family. But since she was now living here, she will eventually have to get used to being kiss goodnight and goodmorning as well as reciprocating it. For tonight though, I wouldn't push it. I recognized she needed space and time to get used to all these changes.

"Goodnight, dad." Going to his side, I kissed him on the cheek as well.

"Night, Ang." Kissing me back on the cheeks, my dad walked up to Storm, shook his hand and bid him goodnight.

At this point, I wasn't surprised by my dad and Storm's friendship. These two seemed to have made a pack when they were alone by the kitchen's threshold. What shocked me, though, was my mom giving Storm the official permission to address her as Elize instead of ma'am before following my dad to the room. Storm had totally bewitched and charmed my parents in a matter of hours. To say I was impressed would be a major understatement.

Sneaking up behind me once my parents were completely out of sight, Storm grasped me around the hips and pulled me into him. My back pressed against his chest, I suppressed a laugh; only letting a small giggle to escape my mouth.

"Storm, what are you doing? My parents can walk in here at any minute." With his strong arms clasped around my upper waist, I tilted my head and looked up at him.

His hot breaths tickling the side of my face "Let them see us." With a sly smile, Storm knew I was enjoying his embrace too much to fight him on this topic.

"So they can get more ideas about us and our relationship... Sure, why not?" My voice laced with sarcasm, I internally rolled my eyes at Storm. The consequence of his carelessness could definitely cost us a few sleepless nights.

Tightening his embrace around my waist, "You should stop worrying so much about what others say or think about you or the people in your life."

"It's not others, Storm. It's my parents." I gently clarified. By now, Storm knew my parents' opinions really mattered to me.

"Even better." Nuzzling his nose in the crook of my neck, his lips touched my skin, leaving a tingling sensation in its wake. "This is your chance to prove to them how much you've changed. You are a warrior; a strong, independent, intelligent and smart woman. Show them this beautiful and fascinating side of you, Doc. Don't take shit from anybody; not even family." The man knew how to get a woman all tingling, warm and fuzzy on the inside. His words touched me to the bone, creating a surge of confidence within me.

"Are you trying to get into my pants with all these heart-warming words?" Doing my best to ignore his smile against my neck, I raised a fine delicate eyebrow at Storm and pulled my lips into a small smile.

"Babe, I don't need to try. – I am getting into those pants tonight. There is no escaping it." Turning my own joke against me, I flushed at Storm's bluntness.

Hopefully, my parents were in their closed room and unable to hear Storm. Or I was screwed big time, and not in the excellently delicious literal way.

"You are horrible, Storm."

Closing his mouth against my ear, "You have no idea just how horrible I can be, yet." He huskily whispered and gently bit down on my earlobe.

"But tonight you are going to get a glimpse." Sliding his right hand from my waist down to my hips, he stopped on my buttocks. Applying pressure on my butt cheek and licking the spot of my earlobe he had bitten, I purred like a cat.

His words, combined with his touch and tongue, left me wanting more. The fire I had successfully killed by accidentally slicing through my finger and having a family dinner, instantly rekindled. It must have been the danger of being seen by my parents because the fire burned brighter than before.

Teasing me, Storm retook my earlobe between his teeth before stepping back. "I would advise you to inform your parents about the possibility of loud music coming from your room while we will be working."

Turning to Storm, confused, "Loud music?"

We've used music to work a case before, and it had worked just as wonderfully as without the background noise. Having the music so loud that it would pierce through my partly soundproof wall, however, was never a thing. After all, noises or sounds could barely make it out of my room.

"I know exactly how loud you cry in pleasure when you come, Angel." Smirking, Storm watched as my face turned deep red.

"That's only with you." I muttered, however, not low enough for him to not hear.

Approaching his lips to my ears again, "Well, Doc, tonight your screams are going to be much louder, I can promise you this. Now, if you don't want to muffle it, that's fine with me. I love hearing your cries of ecstasy. But imagine what your poor parents would think if they hear your cries. Or the sound of me smacking you until your pretty ass turns deep red."

Out of word, I gawked at Storm like a hawk. This guy was so going to be the death of me.

Walking past me, he effectively slapped my butt, jolting me back to the moment. Fishing for his keys inside his jacket hanging on the wall, he winked at me.

"I'm gonna retrieve the case file from my trunk. You better get your ass to your parents' room and inform them." Grinning at me, Storm closed my front door behind him.

Maybe I should just lock him out. Then we'll see how he would deliver his punishment on my poor behind. This awesome idea, however, flew away just as quickly as it came. Storm had a key to the house and pulling the interior manual lock would mean a future worse punishment.

"Sorry, little friend. You're gonna have to endure what's coming. Blame my hormones and my big mouth." Gently patting my buttocks, I lowly mumbled under my breath.

Walking to my parents' room, I quietly tapped on their door. Pushing down my nervousness and pulling my poker face, I explained my possible loud music situation. As someone out there must have said; music is the source of inspiration, aspiration, ideas and creativity.

Gratefully, I wasn't required to explain myself. They seemed to have eaten up the lie of me needing loud music because of the high complication and pressure on the case. Heck, they barely questioned me and went back to sleep.

9

"You've informed your parents?"

Taking yet another sip of my wine, I followed Storm's every movement. Sitting on my leather office chair by my wooden office table, the sounds of the locks latching made my heart jump a beat. To my ears, the sound was equal to the loud 'bong' of a church bell.

"Relax, Doc. I'm not going to eat you." Grinning, he kept the folders on my table.

Looking up at me, "Actually, I stand corrected. I am going to eat you." Dropping my jaw at his word, I was more than convinced the man was evil.

"But I won't kill you, so don't worry." Winking, he got me blushing.

The wine which was supposed to help me get through my punishment turned out to be my biggest enemy. It rose my aptness of getting flustered much quicker.

"You are extremely prude with your words." I finally managed to vocalize.

Turning on my Spotify, Storm selected our usual pop playlist and increased the sound to a reasonably high volume. "I don't see you or your body complaining." Whirling towards me, he raised a brow and smirked with confidence.

"Whatever." Losing this one battle, I rolled my eyes at him. At the end of the day, I was going to win the war.

"Let's go over this case before your impending punishment."

Walking around me, Storm took his seat on the chair beside mine. This time, however, my attention shifted on the glinting metal of the cuff sticking out of his back pocket. Not on my impending doom, he was cheerfully announcing. I could swear his cuffs were not with him this whole night, I would have noticed.

Swallowing, "Why do you have your cuffs with you?" I asked the most obvious question.

When we were undercover in the BDSM dungeon, I used to think how stupid and dumb it was for the newbies to ask their dominant the most obvious questions, but here I was in their place, experiencing the same default in proper questioning.

"It's a little something for you tonight." Purposely placing the cuffs on the table, in my line of view, "But for now, the case." Pushing the file in my hands, Storm was having a blast teasing me and making me nervous.

This prolonging of impending physical punishment and teases about it was without any doubt part of his cruel punishment process. I genuinely pity any submissive who gets him as a dominant or one like him. It was pure torture. The wait. The sight of my restraint propelling my brain to imagine my body bound and restraint.

Doing my best to ignore the cuffs Storm had pushed at the far end of the table while going through the details of the file with me, I concentrated on finding clues. Having a breakthrough on this one-week long case was far more critical than my issues and need to clutch onto control.

My life was funny that way. With Dylan, I had no control, nor had it in me to look for it. After Dylan, I gained control, so much so, it has become a struggle for me to let go. My defence mechanism was clinging onto control as if it was a life source and letting go would mean my death. – And here I am shrinking myself rather than the biography of the suspects and victim in front of me.

Placing his firm strong hand on my thigh, "Doc, stop worrying so much. I'll take care of you."

Listening to his calm, reassuring tone, I let out a breath I didn't know I was holding. Searching his deep green-greyish eyes, I was more than convinced of the truth behind his words. I trusted

Storm to take care of me.

Then something hit me. "Say that again." Ideas swirling inside my head, the wheels started turning like a race car taking off on a racetrack.

"Stop worrying. I'll take care of you?" Confused, Storm simply repeated.

"Worry ... That's it, Storm ... How could I have missed it?" Sarcastically chuckling at my own stupidity for not finding the answer earlier, I was sure I looked and sounded crazy. Storm's puzzling stare was proof enough.

"Okay, what's up, crazy woman?" Giving up on trying to find the answer on his own, Storm posed.

"The case, you dumbo. It's not about the money. It's about worry."

"I'm listening." Professional Storm poked its head as he tried to see from my perspective.

"You might not like where the answer brings us. But we've established Mrs Hearth had over a million-dollar life insurance on her. Naturally, our first theory would be to follow such a big amount of cash. This option, however, only brings us to the husband as he is the direct beneficiary for everything."

"Mr Hearth is the most promising suspect, yes. We will be questioning him again this week. At the station this time." Absentmindedly stroking his chin with his forefinger and thumb, Storm declared.

"I would hold off on that if I were you."

Picking up the piece of paper from the third folder, I wheeled my chair closer to Storm. Pointing at the small note from Mrs Hearth's previous doctor, "What we haven't considered is the woman's last doctor report. Last time she checked at the doctor was when she had an accidental sleeping pill overdose."

Filing through the second folder, I took another sheet and placed it on top of the last document. "Here. This record shows an entry of Mrs Hearth visiting a psychiatrist as per doctor notice. But she attended for only a short period, then nothing."

"She could have gotten better. There's nothing suspicious about it." Looking up at me, Storm couldn't see my point yet.

"Storm, the woman visited the shrink for 2 weeks for 1 hour ... – I don't care how great of a shrink someone claims to be, but healing a woman like Mrs Hearth and solving all her problems; marital included does not take only 2 weeks. Any psychiatrist in their right mind would still have her under observation and therapy."

"Okay, Miss Shrink. We would question the less competent shrink this week." Holding his hands up in surrender, Storm mused.

"Get a warrant for all of Mrs Hearth documents while you are at it. Or that shrink of hers might throw the patient-doctor confidentiality bullcrap at us even though the woman is already dead." Picking up the paper with the notes from her previous doctor at the public hospital downtown, I reread it.

"As you wish, boss." Returning to his serious posture, "Is there anything else I should know? Like the part, I might not like."

"I'm suspecting the son but let me get more definitive proofs before I throw anyone under the bus. – Just, have an officer keep an extremely close watch on the father and son."

"Way not to worry me or ignite curiosity within me."

Lightly laughing, "Curiosity kills the cat, Storm."

"You don't say." Helping me clean up my table, we packed all the documents.

"It's going in my safe, besides your gun for when you need it." Walking away with all the folders I securely kept it in my safe, inside my wardrobe, and locked it in. With all the people in my house, leaving official records and investigation documents in the open was dangerous.

Pivoting back to Storm, all laughter vanished from me. Standing by my bed with a mischievous smirk, he held the handcuffs in front of me. Mentioning for me to walk up to him, I slowly swallowed. Hard. But I complied. The look in his eyes, demanding for my obedience.

"Hands."

His single controlled word held so much power, I found myself holding my hands out for him without a second thought. Tonight

I was finally going to get a glimpse of the dominating side of Storm Ives. Instead of the almost docile, calm, patience, loving and relax Storm. Personally, I had no idea how I felt about it. And this scared me more than anything else.

Not knowing what will happen. If I am going to hate it or worst, like it. If I'll break and finally give my whole self away to Storm. Oh my gosh, what will I do if I am unable to stop myself from breaking my own rules? Having sexual intercourse in its entirety with Storm has after all been one of my deepest and darkest desires. I've seen his thick and long manhood. I've touched it. Felt its power around my fingertips. Stroke it. Tasted it. And sucked it.

"You're overthinking again, Doc. Just concentrate on me, my voice, my touches, and the sensation of your body."

Settling the handcuffs around my wrists, his pool of green captivated me. Snapping the cuffs, the metallic click of the handcuff bonded my ability to freely separate or move my hands. I was now trapped.

10

Taking Storm's advice, I made an exceptional effort to block the noise inside my head. Locking all my attention on Storm, I observed his every movement and waited.

Slipping his hand under my hair, Storm seized the back of my neck. Capturing me in his searching pool of green with a tint of grey, he dipped forward and imprisoned my lips with his. Gently massaging my bottom lip, I relaxed against his slow kiss and welcomed his trailing hand on my back. His masculine scent tantalizing my nose.

Wanting to touch him as well, I moved my hand from between us to only realize I couldn't go far. My hands had little to no free reign. Clasping his strong and firm grip around my curvy waist, Storm pulled me further into him and out of my racing thoughts.

With my arms stuck between our chests, I grabbed the front of his shirt and pressed into the kiss. Holding the kiss, Storm kept his lips locked onto mine. Slowly and sensually relishing the softness of my lips. Purring against his slow torturous kiss, I was already craving for more.

Biting on my slightly swollen lips, Storm gradually and hesitantly let go. Heaving deeply, desire swirled inside Storm's eyes as it swirled within me. Gaping at Storm and his bulging manhood, I could hear my own heart beating. The blood rushing to my ears and my face burning up. I was already feeling hot and in need.

My lower belly was fluttering like a million butterflies were having a dancing party inside. My nipples were thickly stiffened and were brushing against the material of my bra. My womanhood was tingling and yearning Storm's touch.

Glancing between my cuffed hands and Storm, "I wanna touch you, Storm ..... uncuff me, please." Batting my long thick lashes at him, accenting my dilated pleasure-filled pupils, I hoarsely requested.

Taking one of my hands in his, Storm trailed his fingers over the cuff and its outline around my wrist. Peering up at me, he kissed the back of my hand and the footprints his fingers had taken along my wrist. This sight on its own was erotic and mind-numbing. "You are not allowed to touch me until I tell you so."

Gaping at him in astonishment and heightened surprise, "What?"

"You heard me. - No touching or I spike up your punishment."

The asshole was serious. I couldn't believe this. He gets to touch me to his heart's desire, and I'm restraint. Not allowed to touch. Perhaps I should punish him for punishing me. Sounds like a lovely idea, except for the fact that he was the trained dominant in this game.

"Any complaints, Doc?" With a devious grin and darken green eyes, Storm taunted me.

"No." Swallowing my complaints, I recognized Storm had the upper hand.

"That's what I thought." Kissing me on the cheek, Storm teased while unknotting the strings of my sweatpants.

Gulping, I watched Storm crouch to his knees. Gliding my sweatpants down at a snail pace, he smooches a line of long-drawn-out kisses along his path. Gasping, I bit down on my lower lip and fisted the hem of my T-shirt in an attempt to not touch Storm. His lips moving along my inner and outer thigh; along my calf and the entire length of my legs, I wasn't sure how long I could remain standing. My need to touch him was spiralling, and there was only so much I could do to control my instinct.

"Step out." Catching my attention with his domineering and commanding tone, I did as asked.

I couldn't believe how cool and collected he seemed. I was already a hot mess and out of control. Getting back up on his feet, all I could do was thank God my damn sweatpant was finally off. A few more minutes of his soft lips and gliding hot hands on my skin and I would have gone against his order.

"Put your arms up and keep them there. If it falls before I bring it down myself, I amplify your punishment."

"Okay." Following his commanding instruction, I held my arms in the air and waited. With the increasing and swelling pool of wetness between my legs, I was more than ready to do as asked. Especially when his assertive tone and controlled orders were making my inside throb like someone was beating on a tambour.

Squatting halfway in front of me, Storm leisurely hoisted my T-shirt. Doing the same as he did when removing my sweatpants, he kissed his way from my waist to my sides, along my abdomen and cleavage before fully pulling the T-shirt off of me. Leaving me in my bra and panties, he returned his fiery kisses to my neck and skimmed down to the hollow space between my shoulder and neck.

Licking and smacking his mouth on my shoulder blade, he drifted upward to my chin, my jawline and cheeks. Over 50 per cent of my body now covered with his kisses, I would have even bet on love-bites in places where it could easily be hidden.

Kissing my body like he was making out with my lips, my pleasurable moans turned into whimpers. Breaking away from me, Storm once again knew what my body needed.

Profoundly peering into the brown of my eyes, "Walk to your bed's footboard. Look straight. Spread your legs. Bend over and keep your ass up." Stepping away from me, Storm commanded in the utmost controlled and potent tone I've heard.

Positioning myself as instructed without putting up any fight, I stood by. Sensing Storm's eyes on me as he moved around behind me, I had to force myself to not blatantly disobey and look back at what he was doing. Then again, my curiosity and anxiousness were really killing me and my ability to stand tight. Thankfully, my misery was put at rest just as my itchiness for control was starting to take over.

Conscious of Storm's hot breath fanning the back of my neck, I was starting to have this distinct feeling he knew exactly how to work my body. He seemed to know precisely when I can't hold any longer. When my need for his touch becomes beyond desperate. Or how much my body could take before giving up, better than I did.

Storm was testing my ability to let go of control and power. At this point, I wouldn't put it past him to be doing all this to break my defence mechanism. This was just who Storm Ives was. Always looking out for me, even when I am not. Sometimes, I just hate how much Storm cares for me. He was purposely making me fall in love with him, and I truly despised him for that.

Closing his lips to my ear, he clutched a handful of my hair into his fist and tugged. Tugged so hard, I loudly gasped, and my head rose into the air.

"As promised Doc, I won't go hard on you for tonight, but I won't go as easy as I had initially planned either. Not after your teasing stunt in the kitchen. I know you are aware of how this BDSM relationship works. You've attended the initiation classes with me during our investigations. I am your dominant, but this relationship is one of erotic power exchange; not one person having absolute power over another." Releasing my hair, my head fell back to its original position.

Skimming his slender fingers on my back, his touch was light as a feather and somewhat ticklish. Not ticklish enough to be uncomfortable and make me laugh. But enough to heighten my breathing and relax my clenching on the bed.

Playing with the back of my bra and teasingly pulling onto the hook, "Do you remember the actual meaning of BDSM, Angel?"

Gulping at the dominating seriousness behind his voice, I nodded in affirmation. Looking straight ahead, I was scared words were a concept far gone from my head.

Stretching the band of my bra outward, I felt the frame and cup of the bra tighten and dig into my skin. "Use your words, Doc." Mercilessly releasing the band, it harshly and loudly smacked against my back.

Yelping in surprise, I fisted the cover over my bed, "I do." I briskly answered with a low growl.

"What is it?" Hooking the band under his forefinger, "And with less attitude this time."

Feeling Storm stretch the damn band again, I mentally braced myself. "It means Bondage and Discipline, Dominance and Submission, master and slave."

Slowly setting the band back against my reddened back, "Good girl."

Laying a stream of gentle kisses around the band of my bra, "Do you remember the safe word we came up with while undercover?"

My lips slightly pulled up at the memory of how we stupidly came up with our safe word. "Scorpion." Keeping my laughter to myself, I simply stated.

Storm didn't deserve to laugh after striking me with my own bra's band. He was being an asshole. Flickering his tongue on my back, I instinctively arched towards him. An asshole who was doing a great job at working my body, I must admit.

"Use that word when you seriously can't take any more, and I'll stop everything. We don't know your hard limits yet, so we can try anything you want. Just, don't let your fear rule you."

Finally unhooking my bra, he ran his lips and tongue along the track the band marked on my back. "This new path isn't just for my pleasure, Doc."

Keeping his mouth running on my back, Storm coasted one of his hands down to my buttocks. Stroking my butt, "Yes, I badly wanna smack your beautiful ass. But, the end goal is to vanquish your proneness to being fearful, especially to new and unknown territory. It is to help you learn how to let go of absolute control. To trust someone so much, you aren't afraid to love again. To destroy all those baggage, you insist on carrying. To burn anything that dares scare you. And to teach you some much-needed discipline."

Holding my breath, I was having a hard time concentrating on his words with his touches on my behind. I could comprehend each word he uttered. I could feel it pulling at my heart. I could feel myself loving it. At the same time, I could feel his touches churning desires within me. Each stroke alleviating my breathing. The power arousing from him, making me wetter than before. - No wonder I was confused. I could barely decide which feeling and sensation I should concentrate on.

Retracting his strokes from my butt cheeks, he sensually slipped my bra straps from my shoulders and along my arms. Gliding his soft touches to my wrists, Storm let my bra fall with a small 'thud'.

"How should you address me while I'm in control, Doc?"

Gaping at my blue bra laying on top of my cuff; his puffing against my face causing blazing turmoil inside me, "I should address you by sir." Remembering all the explanation and details during the initiation meeting at the BDSM club, I mumbled.

Laying a quick kiss on my cheek, Storm backed away again. His constant coming close and retreating back was really starting to drive me crazy. "If this were an exam, Angel, you would ace it."

"Thank you, sir." Recalling quite clearly what the other submissives would do to gain favour in their dominant's eyes, I copied them.

Fiddling with the waistband of my blue thong, "As much as it pleases me to hear what you just said," he pulled on my thong, the thin material splitting my throbbing wet clit, "I'm onto the game you are playing."

SMACK

Yelping at the single slap on my butt cheek, I instinctively fastened my grip on the bed. It was so sudden, I almost fell face-first on the bed.

"Next time, Doc, keep in mind that I know you."

SMACK

Sucking my breath and string of cuss words, I stayed still.

"Play another mind trick on me, Angel, and your punishment will consist of more than just a few slaps and lashes." Caressing where he had just slapped, he soothed the burning feeling on my butt cheeks.

11

Swallowing, "Yes, sir. I'm sorry, sir."

Gosh, I wasn't stupid. Two slaps and I utterly understood his warning. No more psychological mind tricks on Storm Ives. Not unless I intentionally wanted to get smack.

"I'm glad I'm being understood." Pressing kisses along my spin, he made his way up to my shoulder.

"Arch your back, even more, Doc. Tighten your grip on the sheets. Hold onto your footing and prepare yourself for your awaiting punishment." Brushing his fingers along my back and down to my butt, he instructed far more composed than me.

My chest rising and falling in anticipation, I obediently carried out his order. Seizing hold of my inner thighs, Storm moved my legs apart. Ass high up. Legs opened up for his view and touch. I suddenly felt naked, even though I was still in my panties.

Messing with my psych and endocrine gland, Storm pulled his hands away from my firm round butt cheeks every few seconds. Instead of spanking me as expected, he would increase the teasing by continually fondling my ass. However, it took no genius to figure out he was purposely driving me crazy.

"As your dominant tonight, Doc, it is my responsibility to make sure you are completely aware of why you are being punished."

Startling me, his palm connected with my skin, stinging and vibrating my cheeks as he warmed my bottom. Returning to a caress, "Do you know why you are getting spank tonight, Angel?"

Whacking my ass again, I clenched into the sheets, my breaths laboured. "Yes, sir."

Massaging where he had smacked, "Tell me." He commanded.

"I blatantly disobeyed - OUCH! -" Taking another fervent unexpected hit, I bumped forward and strongly fisted the sheets.

Striking without the kneading, he's been performing, "Did I ask you to stop?"

"No, sir. I apologize."

Slugging his hand on my tingling chafed ass, "Apologies accepted. Keep talking."

Another cracking thump, "Tell me what you've done." One more slap, "How did you land yourself in this position?"

Sucking in my ragged breathing after yet another harsh swipe, "I chose to disobey your direct order - AHH! - and warn - Ouch- ing, sir." Giving me a hot prickling bottom, my sentence broke from his fervent unforgiving strikes.

"What else?" Pulling his arm back and puissantly clipping my ass, Storm showed his dissatisfaction towards my non-descriptive answer.

"I teased you on purpose, sir. Knowing you couldn't do anything because of my parents' presence." Crashing his lips on my stark red button, Storm soothed the sting and rewarded my correct answer.

"And?" Biting on my ass cheeks, I let out a growl.

His touches, lips, tongue and teeth grazing against my burning inflamed skin gave rise to pleasure within me. Racking my brain for an answer, all I got was a smudge of dots. "I can't remember, sir."

Backhanding my ass, this time I was prepared for it. Nonetheless, my scream was just as loud as when I wasn't prepared for his hits.

"Try harder, Doc."

"I don't - Darn it!" Exhaling a sharp breath, I cussed at his swift swipes.

"This attitude, Angel, is gonna get you the belt. I warned you about your attitude earlier ... Didn't I?" Petting my poor afflicted ass, Storm's high-octane compelling voice and statement rose my breathing to a whole new level.

The throbbing and wetness between my legs soaring and piquing its interest at the news. I should be getting anxious at the idea of being belted, not excited and aroused. Surely something was broken inside me.

"Yes, sir. You did. I'm sorry, sir." Pinning down my excited hormones, I concentrated on the pain instead. Not on the pleasure in the pain.

Sensing Storm taking a slight step back from me, all my sensory processors kicked in and went on overdrive. Hearing him take off his shirt, my heart slightly picked up. Given the situation and position I was in, I seriously couldn't be blamed for wanting to see, touch and trace Storm's bare muscular chest, abs or biceps. Detecting the sounds of fiddling and belt unlooping, my heart quickly jumped. Forgetting all about the earlier small elevation of heartbeats.

"Sir? ... What are you doing?" Not even daring to look back, I rasped. The suspense killing me.

Hearing him fasten the belt around his hand, "Demonstrating what happens to girls who show attitude."

Letting out a guttural cry, the lashing of his leather belt connected with my sore bottom a couple of times.

"And disobey direct and clear orders." Swinging his arms zealously, the scourging of the belt marked me.

"Sir ... UGGH... sir, please ...ahh! ... I ... OW! Can't... please, sir - OUCH ... Stop."

Clinging to the bed as if it were my life source, I didn't think I could withstand his belting and retain composure. I could feel myself breaking under his hands and severe afflictions.

Bowing forward and capturing a fistful of my hair, Storm pulled my head to his lips. "If you really believe this much punishment is all you deserve, say the safe word, and I'll stop everything ... Just say the word, Angel ... Otherwise, I continue." Unflustered and cool, Storm gave my flustered and burning self a choice.

Those arduous whipping of his were painful. I wanted him to stop abusing my newly redden ass. But was this much punishment really enough? Did I deserve more after purposely taunting him?

After gleefully sexually frustrating him? Should I take all the punishment he deems necessary? Particularly after the sadden and frustrated glaze in his eyes every time I get him hard and refuse to let him fuck me as he so desires.

"I deserve the punishment, sir ... Please continue, sir." My voice cracking, I made my final decision. This was only right after all my teasing and misbehaviours.

His lips stretching into a smile by my ear, Storm was satisfied and pleased with my answer. Slurping my earlobe between his lips, a shudder ran through my body. Moaning at his nibbling, I arched myself further into him. Ceaselessly fliting the length of my back, his moistened mouth smashed onto my butt. Smudging my tender, inflamed buttocks, a sense of euphoria started to build up inside me.

Drawing up from my dampened ass, "Great answer, Angel."

Stooping low again, he held my butt cheeks between his warm palms. The same palms that were smacking me a few minutes ago. Nibbling on my searing ass, the stinging pain began to turn more pleasurable. Humming with sensual gratification, my wet thong soaked up with my source of pleasure.

Hooking his fingers around the thin material of my thong, Storm peeled it off my ass and down my leg at a snail's pace. Luxuriously prolonging his brushing of lips against my skin on his way, a sense of titillation resonated through me. The nipping, the grazing of his teeth and fingers, as well as, the sensation of his firm yet soft lips was producing a different kind of heat within me.

Sweeping his darting tongue upward, Storm left me open-mouthed. Grabbing my ass again, he separated my cheeks and tongued my butt hole. Jolted and at a loss for appropriate words, I instinctively pushed my ass further into his face.

My core was aching and thrilled, demanding attention, and my hands were itching to be released. To hold onto the back of Storm's head and press him deeper into me. I was desperate to touch him. To run my fingers through his hair. Sighing in need for more and gladness at how his expert tongue was massaging my tight butthole, I opened my legs even more for him.

Sensing the trembling of a future orgasm coursed through me, I braced myself for its heavenly feeling. Dominant Storm, however, was ruthless and absolutely rude.

Groaning, I was clearly displeased when he withdrew his gifted tongue the very moment I got close to exploding in his mouth.

Smacking my cheeks, I was in a daze and grunting. My body was confused. On the one hand, there was the smacking. On the other hand, there were Storm's lips running all over my butt.

"Ahh ... please, sir... Ouch ... please..."

Another belt grazing the creek of my ass and my damp labia, "Please what?"

That was the question of the century. 'Please what?'

Please stop or please continue? I was turned one, in need of him inside me. But I also wanted the lashing to cease. With the number of hits I've gotten, I'm overly confident I won't be able to sit properly tomorrow.

"Storm - OUCH! - I mean, sir ... please me. - I want you, sir." Ragged dense breathing, I groaned and whimpered at the same time.

Crouching down again, Storm's hot lips traced along the glowing imprint his belt and palms had made. Hearing the belt drop from his firm grasp, my heart did a little somersault. My butt was done getting busted by his infernal belt for tonight.

Holding me leg spreads, Storm plunged his sharp tongue in and out my butt a couple of times. "You mean like this?" Teasing me with the idea of finally massaging my inside with his mastered tongue, the raging storm of anticipation within me broke to a new level.

Whining with zest, "Please, sir ... please ... I ... I want - Ooh! - I want your mouth - ahh! Sir ... please ... inside me." Jaggedly crying out my need, I was like a depraved animal. The desire for him was slowly killing me.

Biting on my butt cheeks, I let out a small squeal. With all the noises I was making, I was so glad most rooms in my suite was soundproof, and the music was turned up inside my room.

"Tell me why I should give it to you?" Commanding, authoritative and irresistible, dominant Storm demanded.

I Goddamn deserved it for once. Secondly, I took all those smacks so I could be pleased the way I want at the end of the night. Thirdly, I fucking demanded it - that's why.

"Because I really need it, sir." Wolfing down my sassiness, I gave Storm a more submissive-appropriate answer.

This man should be really grateful I am willing to stoop this low for him during intercourse. Any other man, and it would be me doing the beating - without the pleasure part. Storm Ives was extremely lucky I like him far more than I've ever liked any other men.

Completely going down on his knees, "Just what a man wants to hear."

Playfully spreading the slit of my womanhood, "A man who knows how much effort it took you to bolt down your sassiness and loudly ask for me to please you." Pressing one of his fingers against my clit, Storm redirected his mouth to my butthole and ate me out from behind.

Lustily moaning my "Oohs" and "Ahhs", I ground my ass against his mouth. Lapping two of his fingers inside my front entrance, I felt myself reaching close to my release. A release which was denied to me at least 3 times since we started my punishment.

Grasping hold of my hips with his other hand, Storm kept my shuddering body in place. Thrusting a third finger inside me, my back slightly jolted in surprise. Stroking deeper into my hot dripping sex, I felt myself clenching around his fingers. Whimpering in ecstasy at the diverse sensation of his lapping tongue in my ass and the furious pounding of his fingers inside my vagina, I was all sort of shaken up.

Gripping harder on my bed sheet and pressing forward, I bite onto the cloth of the sheet to tone down my orgasmic cry as I came all over Storm's mouth and fingers. Feasting on every drop of my juices, his lips trailed from my ass to my clit. Super sensitive from all the spanking and earth-shattering orgasm, my ability to stand on my own two feet was near to impossible. Letting most of my weight fall on Storm's firm hold around my waist, my legs had literally turned into jello.

Lifting his head from between my legs, Storm spun me around and pushed me down onto the bed in a flash. Falling on my back, I stared at Storm with wide-eyes. Halfway rising up, he took my cuffed wrists in his hands and rose it above my head.

Staring deep into my brown desire-filled eyes, "How are you holding up?" The concerning aspect of Storm showed up. Momentarily smothering his dominant side. A side which I'll admittedly accept I love as much as his loving, concerning, protective, patient and funny self.

"Other than a sore ass, I am holding fine."

"Pleased to hear my handiwork didn't go to waste." With a smirk, he ran his hands up and down my sides.

12

"Keep your arms up." Leaning forward, Storm caressed my lips with his.

Purring into his mouth, I opened my lips for his darting tongue and legs for his invasive fingers. Bucking my hips to match the tempo of his thrusting, I gleefully took all four of his fingers inside my pools of extreme wetness. Digging my nails on the pillow above my head, the slow love-making of his fingers was driving me nuts and wild.

Biting down on my lower lip, his mouth joined the same torturous tempo, and his other hand went up, fondling with my breasts. Playing with my stone-hard nipples, he tweaked it between his fingers every now and then. Lowly moaning against Storm's mouth, I was at the mercy of his touch. Overflow with heat, my body rocked against his probing, the passion within me seeping off. Burning for him, Storm was my only deliverance.

Feeling the same shudder as before stream through my core to my tiptoes, I pressed my entire self into Storm. Knowing exactly what my body needed and when it needed it, Storm smashed his fingers deeper and faster into me. Dropping his lips between the crest of my neck and shoulder, Storm bit down as I did the same on his shoulder. His instruction, after all, was for my hands to not touch him, not other parts of my body.

Pounding harder, he finger-fucked me until I came crashing into his hands once more like an angry wave destroying everything in its passage. Steadily extracting his wet fingers from my sex, Storm ploddingly licked my juices off his fingers. Capturing my gazes with his, my chest sharply heaved for air. The sensuality with which his tongue darted out and erotically wrapped around his fingers covered with my cum augmented my need of him.

Removing his ring finger from his mouth with a loud 'pop', "You wanna know how good you taste?"

Nodding in affirmation, "Yes, sir. I want to have a taste."

I truly did. I wanted to taste myself off of him. Eating up Storm with the power of my mere eyes, I wanted to spill my juices of ecstasy all over his raw power of manhood. I wanted more than just his fingers and mouth inside my sex. But, did I dare go that far with this wonderful man right now? There were so many emotions and tensions between us.

"Aww ... mhm ..." Inserting two of his fingers back into my delicate dripping entrance, I was brought back to the moment the best way possible.

Looking down at me with a mischievous smirk, Storm crooked his fingers inside of me and fervently pumped. Taking more of my climax around his fingers, Storm let it dripped on top of my partly opened mouth before rubbing the remnant all over my lips. "Don't lick, yet." Quickly retracting my tongue from my lips, I was under Storm's domineering spell.

Intaking a harsh breath, my clit engulfed Storm's playful fingers again. Twisting and curling his fingers inside me, my body happily gave Storm more of my ejaculation. Offering me his slick fingers, I opened my mouth and tasted my own release of pleasure and ecstasy.

Two fingers shoved inside my mouth, I let my lips and tongue do their mighty job. "Let go of my fingers, and I restart your punishment." Storm authoritatively commanded.

First off, I had no intention of letting go any time soon. Secondly, another round of punishment was absolutely out of the question for tonight. I could barely feel my buttocks as it was, and I'm pretty sure after what we've done so far tonight, I would be exhausted beyond belief. More belting and I might not wake up tomorrow morning. Pressing my lips around his two fingers, I nodded in approval.

"Good girl. Now, open your legs wide for me." Was the last word I heard from him before he dove his face between my legs again.

My hips grinding and bucking against his mouth, he sucked me completely dry. Moaning and doing my best to continue sucking his fingers, I was finding it hard to not let go. Storm was drinking me up like I was an oasis in a desert and he had been thirsty for weeks. Shaking against his magical lips, my thighs internally boiled up, and I came like a wild animal. For some reason, all the spanking had made me more susceptible to climax with a ferocious intensity.

Removing his fingers from my mouth, he finished cleaning all my cum with his tongue. Hot from the inside-out, my breathing heavy, my heart racing one thousand miles per hour and the flipping inside my belly decreasing, I stayed still under Storm's smooches. Streaming his mouth from my inner thighs to my stomach, to my breasts and on top of my lips, Storm wiped away the residuum of my juices he had rubbed on my lips earlier.

Bringing my cuffed hands forward, he kissed along the outline of the cuffs. Speechless from my multiple consuming orgasms and the sign of him stroking my wrists with his tongue above me, I knew I would never look at those handcuffs the same way ever again. Unclicking those damn handcuffs, I was finally restraint free. Massaging the pink bruise around my wrists with his fingers and tongue, I signed in pleasure. This simple, caring action of his wholly made up for the tight restraint.

Kneading my wrists and hands with his forefinger and thumb, "How are you feeling?"

"Tired and raw. But I'm good."

Getting off me and laying down beside me, "Give me your hand." Compassion and love in his voice instead of authoritativeness and commands, Storm held his hand out for me.

Placing my hand on his open palm, I allowed myself to be dragged on top of him. Pulling the blanket from my bed, he wrapped it around us. Laying flat on top of him, the soft material of the blanket was a fresh relief on my aching ass. The warmth within it, a welcome sensation to my body that was starting to lose heat from all the orgasms. Enclosing his warm athletic arms around my back and waist, he drew circles on my skin. Loving the comfort of his secure embrace, I relaxed in his arms and tenderness.

"You did extremely well, Ang. I love how you didn't use the safeword despite the uncomfortableness you must have felt. Especially with this being your first punishment. I'm really proud of the strength you've shown." With pride and passion glimmering in his eyes, I knew he actually meant every word and wasn't just saying all these as an aftercare as I've observed many dominant do to their subs.

"Thanks, Storm. It was different, deep and colourful in its own way." Nuzzling my chin on the crook of his neck, I maintained eye contact.

"Tell me honestly, Angel, are you still against BDSM and its culture?"

"I was never against BDSM, Storm. I simply had my reserve to that side of the world."

"Do you still have your reserve, then?" With his hands caressing my ass, my decision-making skills were slightly malfunctioning.

Doing my best to ponder over his question while searching his greenish-greyed eyes. "Sincerely, Storm, I don't know yet. I don't have as much reserve as I used to, but I'm not totally sure how I truly feel about all these. I will need more time to answer this one."

"You want me to stop being your dominant then?"

"No. I didn't say that." I responded way too quickly for my own good.

"You just have to say the word, and I'll take back the deal we made." Hiding his smirk, Storm seriously gave me the choice to pull out of this craziness.

But was it really crazy? Haven't I enjoyed it? Giving him total control in bed has only proven fruitful and blissful. And those Goddamn spankings. As much as it has hurt, my body had begun to anticipate it. To longed for it. And to embrace the smacks that vibrated through my cheeks, my skin and core.

"Well now Storm, we don't need to go that far." Discerning the playful glint in his lustful eyes, "I mean ... It's a deal and ... umm... I don't go back on promises that easily." I tried to cover my tracks.

"Babe, if you loved it and enjoyed those smacks, there's no shame

89

in it. Own it." Stroking my back, his smirk grew another inch.

"I never said I loved it. I just said I'm willing to give this thing with you more than one try." I rectify for Detective Storm Ives.

"And I'm willing to give it to you more than once." Playfully swatting my ass, he grinned, a promise in his words.

"You are incorrigible. Maybe it's you who needs to be disciplined."

"I'm plenty disciplined, Doc." Gently rolling me off him, Storm shuffled to his feet.

"Where are you going?" Lying on my stomach, I gazed up at Storm, perplexed.

Had my jesting about him temporarily taking the role of a submissive hurt him? Was he really one of those dominants who refused to participate in an exchange of power? Because if this were the case, this new level of relationship between us wouldn't last long.

"To take a much needed cold shower. My case of blue-ball is getting worse with each word coming out of your beautiful mouth."

Running my eyes over a shirtless Storm, my eyes stopped dead on its tracks the moment it landed on his poking friend. With the zipper and buttons of his dark jeans open, a part of his grey boxer was visible. Licking my suddenly dry lips, Storm was a scrumptious power-emitting sight.

"Stop eye-fucking me, Angel." Following his every movement as he got himself a towel and fresh boxer from his designated drawer in my closet, I felt like a starving animal.

"Care if I join you for a hot shower." Propping myself up, my shoulder holding most of my weight, I supported my head on the back of my steepled fingers.

"Angel..." Hissing under his breath, "You're making this really difficult on me."

Batting my eyelashes at him and pulling my most innocent face; just like Kyle does when he really wants something. "Please ... pretty please."

Slumping his shoulder like the end of the world was in front of him, Storm deeply signed. "You are going to be the death of me,

Angelica Buar." Turning on his back, Storm entered my personal bathroom, leaving the door cracked.

Grinning to myself, I rapidly and giddily got to my feet. Entering the bathroom, the hot water already creating steam inside my square-shaped shower, I slide its glass door and closed it behind me. Creeping up behind Storm who was already drenched in the scorching hot water battering against his body, I wrapped my arms around his torso.

Laying a trail of kisses all over Storm's back, I stood on my tiptoes and grazed my teeth against the curve of his shoulder. Gradually sliding my hands downward, I bit down on the side of Storm's neck, emitting a deep animalistic grunt from him.

"Doc..." His hands flying to the wall in front of him for support, he moaned with a slight controlled voice.

Using my tongue to massage the section I had bitten, I waited until his shoulder relaxed and dug my teeth into the crook of his shoulder. - I wanted him to lose control as I did, damn it.

"Say my name, Storm ... my full first name." Licking the love bite between the space of his neck and shoulder, his control was successfully shattering.

"Angelica."

Seizing his hard erection between my palm, I kneaded his length. Groaning between lustful breaths, my name was beautifully and gutturally spelt out. Kissing his back as a reward, I felt his body go rigid under my lips.

"Keep moaning my name like that, please. It's music to my ears." Moving to the front, I pressed a firm kiss on his lips.

Kneeling down, the hot water like rainfall on my body, I was just as drenched as Storm. My long brown hair stuck to my neck, shoulder and back. Rubbing the tip of his throbbing length, I looked up at Storm, the hot water sticking to my eyelashes. Mouth-agape, chest heaving, desire-filled eyes, his slightly short jet black hair stuck to his forehead, Storm was a majestic view.

Bringing my head lower, I passed my tongue over the underside of his massive cock. Teasing Storm, I playfully grazed my teeth against the base as I wrapped my tongue around his gigantic length. Fondling with his raw potency of power, I was having a hard time filling the whole of him around the small of my hand. But I wasn't going to give up.

Stroking him, I slowly and provocatively took his whole length inside my mouth. Moaning against him, I sucked him like a lollipop. A wonderfully scrumptious lollipop. Gagging and swallowing the whole of him, Storm loudly and throatily growled in ecstasy. Unable to keep his hands on the wall, he fisted my hair and pushed my face further into him.

"Mmmmmm ..." Playing with his balls, my unintelligent and incomprehensible words vibrated against him. The sensation of him between my tingling fingers while the whole of him pounded my mouth was making my inside hot all over again. Not only was the scorching water boiling my skin but the passion and need within me was boiling my interior.

"Shit ... Angelica ..." His moderate volume moaning turned loud, rough and croaky.

Relentlessly driving deep inside my mouth and grunting like a caveman, Storm seriously made me wished he was fucking my womanhood, not just my mouth.

"I'm gonna come." Pressing harder on the back of my head, my hands landed below his navel.

Aware I loved it when he ejaculates inside my mouth, his thrust girthed deeper and furiously. Shaking under my touch, my tongue, my mouth and my sucking, Storm vigorously exploded like a projectile. His cry of pleasure echoing through the walls of the bathroom. Swallowing his release, I continuously drew on his length until he was all clean.

Rising to my feet, I took Storm's face in my palms and passionately kissed him on the lips. His hands fondling my sopping body, I looped my arms around his wet neck and pressed into the kiss under the pouring hot water. The passion in our french-kiss enough to reignite our desires.

Breaking apart for some much-needed air, "Now I can go to bed fully satisfied." Walking around Storm with a wide grin, I slide out of the shower.

"Have fun with your cold shower." Turning the lever under the sink to cold, I bolted out of the bathroom, giggling at Storm's sharp cry of surprise.

13

Towel wrapped loosely around his hips, the 'V' of his pelvic glistening with droplets of water slithering from his partly dry chest, his wet hair all tousled up, Storm was a delicious sight.

"You know Doc, this little act you pulled deserves a whole new round of punishment."

Feigning absolute innocence and stifling an almost involuntary moan at the idea of another round of punishment, my sensitive ass tingled. "I don't know what act you speak of? I was just accommodating your request for a cold shower, sir."

Dressed in my black silk mini kimono robe with its matching short black silk nightgown, I remained sprawled on my belly, on my soft bed and watched Storm's every movement like a hawk.

"Keep teasing, woman."

Successfully drying his dark hair, he threw his wet towel inside the hamper and prowled towards me with a hungry look. The man was a dishevelled caveman; a walking sex God and a neurochemical catalyst.

"And those silks you are wearing would become your new restraint. I'll even go as far as using it to gag you. And that silky belt around your waist will tie your legs in whatever position I want, for however long I want." Crawling on the bed, Storm pulled me forward by the legs and settled himself on either side of my thighs.

Yelping in surprise, I gazed up at a bare chest Storm. In only his briefs, he leaned forward, his hands untying the silk belt of my kimono robe, "What do you say, Doc?"

Skilfully opening my robe with his slender fingers and delicately sliding it off my shoulder, my breathing and sexual arousal spiked up. The gentleness and deftness with which his fingers grazed my skin made the dirty words he was uttering so much more sensual.

"I'll say I'm willing to let you do to me whatever you deem necessary, sir." I hoarsely mumbled, enjoying his lingering touches on my shoulder blades, cleavage and neck.

"Is that so?" Taunting me, I could feel my skin tingle under his touch and the fire cracking up inside me.

Batting my eyelashes at Storm, "Yes, sir, absolutely."

Pleased with my answer, Storm crashed his lips against my skin, outlining the same pattern his fingers were tracing.

"I'll gladly take you up on this promise." Getting off me and moving to the head post of the bed. "But I'll have to take a rain check. You are already too sore and tired for tonight. The last thing I want is to push you too far too soon."

Completely sliding off my silk kimono robe and neatly placing it on the bedside table, I took Storm's outstretched hand.

"How considerate of you." Snuggling against his firm chest, he pulled the cover over us.

Tightening his hold around my arm and pushing me deeper into him, "I'm always extremely considerate when it comes to you, Angel. If you were any other sub, you would be spread out with your ass up and bonded in a Japanese knot right now. You would be at my complete mercy, and I would be whipping you so hard, you will be parched from crying for leniency, but you will get none. Your whole body would be marked and imprinted with my belt, the metal head shredding your ass like no tomorrow and the idea of pulling the trick you did in the bathroom would forever vanish from your system."

Swallowing hard and long, "Does this mean I can't prank you as much as I desire anymore? I mean ... would I always have to live by certain rules or risk being punished?"

Tracing patterns on my arms, Storm's eyes bored into me. "The answer would be a definite yes ... if you were any of my other subs. But you, Angelica, are not. You are far more special and precious to me. As painful as your sexual teasing can be, I wouldn't in a million year want to change your mischievous attitude. What I would want to change is your need for maximum control, your tendency to let your fear rule your life and your lack of discipline. But, babe, at the end of the day, I truly do like you the way you are."

Ferociously nailing the flapping of my heart, I took a deep breath in an attempt to hold down my heart. **DO. NOT. FALL. IN. LOVE. WITH. THE. MAN. ANGELICA BUAR. I repeat, DO. NOT. FALL. FOR. HIM.**

Cautiously seeping in his amorous and passionate gaze, my resolution and continuous mental repetition to not fall for Storm was slowly taking a dive. But what my betraying heart did not know was that I was adamant and strong-minded. I was going to keep being a friend and maintain our relationship as it is; no matter how much it was slowly killing me.

"Does this mean we can still be all vanilla? I don't mind trying this BDSM scene with you, but I also do like the usual simple scene." Asking one of the most important questions of the night, I expectedly look at Storm.

"We can definitely do both, Angelica. One crucial aspect of this new level of intimacy in our relationship is open judgement-free communication. It is essential we are comfortable to ask whatever we want and not be afraid to speak our mind if something is bothering either of us. Absolute honesty and trust is the basis of all relationship; especially one in the BDSM world."

"Okay, I can roll with that." Smiling at Storm, I relaxed against his touches and laid my head back in the crook of his neck.

"Speaking about open communication, are you finally going to tell me what happened in New Hampshire? How come your parents are now living here? Where's your brother?"

My blissful, relaxing moment cut short, I began recounting the whole story of what I had found out and how I had reacted. Kissing me on the forehead and strengthening his grip around me, I was grateful Storm didn't think I acted stupidly and impulsively.

He even went as far as sharing my anger and frustration. Not only was he extraordinarily supportive but was also acting as if my parents were his. At that moment, my desire to give in my love for him and accept his previous proposal of us being an actual couple was ravingly eating at me.

Then again, I knew I couldn't give in to this scary desire of mine. At least, not yet. Engulfed in Storm's embrace, I fell asleep in no time. The issue with my brother and parents long forgotten.

~~ | | ~~

"Mommy mommy wake up!"

Grumbling my resistance under my breath, I tried to ignore Kyle's insistent poking on my arm and snuggle deeper into Storm. I was too tired and sore to be moving around just yet. But Kyle wasn't taking no for an answer. He was as stubborn and resilient as his mother.

Climbing on my bed like a little monkey, he forcibly crawled between Storm and me. Giggling to himself, Kyle nestled between the small spaces he had made like a puppy.

Wrapping his long, strong arms around me, with Kyle nuzzling up against him, "Good morning, mommy's alarm clock, how was your sleep?" Storm groggily mused.

"It was great. - Grandpa made a yummy breakfast for me."

The hyped-up energy oozing off Kyle was making me even more tired. I just wanted a peaceful quiet Sunday where I could sleep in. But that was just a dream at this point.

"Boys, take it somewhere else. Some people still want to sleep." Grunting, I turned my back to them and covered my face with the blanket.

Penchant over my shoulder and staring at my covered face, "But mommy, it's already nine o'clock."

"So." Mumbling under the blanket, my attempts to tune them out was miserably failing.

"Kyle, do you wanna play a game." Sensing Storm shifts his weight on the bed, I knew he had something Machiavelli up his sleeves.

"Yes, yes." Shifting his attention away from me, Kyle concentrated on Storm.

"Let's play tickle mommy until she screams game." Jumping up and down on my bed, Kyle excitedly agreed with Storm.

Bracing myself for their attacks, I firmly locked my hold on the blanket around me. Storm and his obsession with making me scream were cruel. As if last night was not enough, he also had to work my parched throat first thing in the morning.

"Guys, stop ..." Giggling, I tossed around under their fervent tickling assault.

"I swear, I'm gonna kill both of you if you don't stop." Kicking away, my pleads were being unheard.

"Kyle ... Storm ... please..." I tried one last time. My body was shaking and giving away under their torturous fingers. My state of soreness wasn't helping my case either.

"Okay Kyle, I think mommy had enough for today." Retreating back, Storm got off the bed and dressed up in his running clothes.

"I hate you guys." Grumbling, I pulled the cover around my chest.

"And we love you too, right, Kyle." Widely smiling, Storm high-fived Kyle.

I knew Storm means it in a friendly way, but does he even realize how much those words coming from his mouth affects me. It makes my heart flutter, increases the sweaty feeling in my palms, and blank out my mind for a mild second.

"Yes, mommy, we love you." Pulling my attention back, Kyle sweet innocent voice made up for those torturous tingling I was inflicted.

"Good morning, Elize, Auden." Storm casually greeted my parents.

Promptly looking towards my room entrance, I profusely blushed; my face a picture-perfect of a deer in the headlights. Resting against the trim of my doorway, their eyebrows raised with immense interest and a smile plastered on their faces, there was no doubt they've stood there from the moment Kyle walked into the room.

"Good morning, son." My dad usual soft voice sounded booming to my petrified ears.

98

"Morning, Storm." My mom lightly greeted Storm, her tone way too pleasant.

Playfully winking at me, Storm closed the bathroom door behind him, leaving me alone to face the music. The winked look decorating his face like icing on a devil cake telling me he was enjoying my embarrassment to the entirety.

"Morning, mom, dad." Brushing aside the glint shimmering in their eyes, I knew they were already reading too much into what they saw.

"Morning, Angel." They simultaneously greeted. I must have still been under the fog of my sleep because their voices together sounded like an echo of death to me.

"I'm so glad you were actually dressed under that blanket. I was almost afraid I would see you naked if you moved."

"DAD!" I screeched in horror.

"I wouldn't blame you if you weren't. Have you seen the man's body? ... Uh, and that chest of his ... umm... - A scrumptious piece of cake."

Lingering her eyes at the closed door, my face burned up like a blazing roast at my mom's open admiration of Storm's exquisite body. A body which was all over me last night.

"Wait! You're sure you're straight, right? - Because there's no way you would find me fully clothed if this man was in my bed."

"MOTHER! - I am perfectly straight."

If I thought I was burning up earlier, my face now resembled an erupting volcano. This was probably how I would die. Out of embarrassment. My gravestone would probably read 'Dr Angelica Buar, death by extreme blushing.'

"What, just asking? The guy is the perfect picture of a sex God." Throwing her hands up in surrender, she professed, not even apologizing.

"Hey, I'm right here. You know, the guy you married and swore faithfulness to until death does us apart." Jumping in, my dad mused.

"Don't worry, babe. I still love you and no sex God in the entire universe is ever going to steal me from you." Kissing my dad on the lips, she silenced him.

"Ewe... Go make out somewhere else."

Gross, I didn't need to see my parents make out. I don't care how old I was, this image has never been appealing to me.

"What? You mean this?" Circling his arms around my mom's waist and back, my dad dived into a round of French-kiss with my mom. Watching her being pressed against him like a sandwich and passionately exchanging saliva was so much worse than hearing her purr under his lips.

"Come here, Kyle. You don't need to see or hear this disgusting thing." Covering Kyle's eyes with my hand, I curled us up in a ball and hid our faces under the blanket.

"But mommy, you and Storm do the same thing?" Whispering against my embrace, I was so Goddamn ecstatic we had a blanket under our head, and his whisper was muffled.

"Shush, Kyle. Never ever repeat this to anyone. That's a secret between Storm, me and you. Okay." Whispering in my mommy-tone, I made sure Kyle got my point.

"Okay, mommy." The innocent child simply agreed with no further question. Kyle was so cute, and I was so proud at how he always has my back; even at five years old.

"Well, I got out at a perfect time, I see." Closing the bathroom door behind him, Storm quipped.

"I was just showing my innocent daughter what it's like to be kissed by someone you love." My mom remarked with witticism, the huskiness in her voice more than evident. The woman was aroused, no doubt about it.

"Does Doc have a love interest I don't know about?" Playing along with my mom, Storm taunted.

"Yes, I have one. Do you mind?" Exclaiming from under the blanket, I was hoping my tone would scare them away so I could be left alone. Just to snuggle with my loving child and relax.

Pulling the blanket off my face, I was consumed by the fire in Storm's eyes as he stared down at me despite the smile on his lips,

"Is that so? - I would love to meet that lucky person."

"Not happening." I sassily bit back with my own smirk.

"That we shall see." Bending forward, Storm pressed a firm kiss on my forehead, "I'll see you all in a bit. I'm going on my run." Giving me one last piercing look, Storm turned on his heels.

"Have fun. Elize and I are going into our room to do some important work with loud music on." Winking at Storm and me with mischievousness, my dad was making reference to last night.

"Try not to disturb." Quickly studying their faces, their darkened eye colours, their pupils dilated and their mischievous grin, it dawned on me what type of work they were pointing at.

'Ewww... Gross...' My brain mentally gagged and screamed. On the outer surface, my facial expression was blank. I couldn't let them know I knew they knew about last night.

"They know." Storm nonchalantly voiced out as soon as my parents vanished from our sight to go do their 'work'.

"Yep." I mechanically responded with a 'pop' at Storm's departing back.

Alone with Kyle in my tight embrace, I laid still and gradually wrapped my head around all that has happened since yesterday. My parents' arrival, them meeting and questioning Storm, them taking an absolute surprising liking of Storm or my first personal step into the BDSM world.

Just reflecting on the punishment I had received caused my ass to prickle. The sound of my own screams reverberating inside my brain. The stinging I had felt last night engraved in my mind forever. Pondering about Storm, about us and about our relationship behind closed doors mixed up with all the relationship and romance stories both my parents recounted last night.

The saying that life can change in a snap of a finger had been just that for me - a saying. Now, it was a living truth, and I had become a victim of its cruelty.

14

Lost in great conversation with my parents while toasting four slices of bread, I was my happiest. After five years of not seeing them in person, I had stopped believing such a blissful moment would come to pass.

Sitting at the kitchen counter with Kyle, my parents threw pleasantries at me and fed me with more stories while I was busy scrambling half a dozen of eggs for mine and Storm's breakfast. Sipping on my hot cup of coffee, I signed in pleasure. The warmth of this black nectar coursing through my used-to-be-parched throat and down my system. The caffeine building up all my lost energy.

After last night and my need to finish some necessary work today, coffee was going to be my best of best friend for the duration of the day. Aware Storm would soon be back from his usual one hour morning run, I began mixing up all the ingredients for Storm's morning smoothie.

"What are you doing?" Looking at me like I was doing something disgusting, my mom asked. "I thought you were in desperate need of solely coffee."

"Oh, I am, mom. This smoothie is not for me."

Right on queue Storm entered the kitchen threshold, sweating like a pig. Huffing and puffing, he seemed to have run a marathon.

"This clean-cut health concoction is for Mr Healthy over there." Pointing my chin forward towards Storm, I shouted over the deafening roar of the blender.

"Something you should definitely try, Miss Unhealthy." Bent forward, hands on his knees, Storm worked on catching his breath and returning his heart rate to normal.

Turning off the blender and making my way to the plate cabinet, "I'll pass, thanks."

I had no desire to be panting like a dog and sweating bullets early in the morning. I was good doing yoga first thing when I wake up. It put things into better perspective, clears my system, revitalises me, and keeps me flexible and strong.

Feeling a shadow behind me and an arm stretched above my head, I was momentarily caught off. "Geez, Storm ... Don't sneak up on me like that." This must have been the hundredth time I've told him this. But does he listen to me ... no! - He apparently is head bent on giving me a heart attack.

"Sorry for trying to save your precious little head from cracking open in the middle of your kitchen." Still holding the wooden cabinet door above my head, the palm of his rugged hand engulfed the edges.

Mentally measuring the angle of my head and its distance from the edge of the cabinet door, it was extremely likely I would have hit my head if not for Storm. Then again, I wasn't one to accept defeat so easily, nor was I going to agree with Storm without an argument.

Turning my head sideways and gazing up at Storm with a confident look that shouted I was right and he was wrong. "Nothing would have happened. I have everything perfectly handled."

Taking two plates out of the cabinet, "Of course, Miss Clumsy and I'm the King of Sweden." Jesting and smirking, Storm handed me the two plates.

"You are impossible. Just go have your shower, you stink of sweat." Walking away from him, I waved my hand in front of my nose for dramatic effect.

"Something which happens when you actually exercise, Doc." Winking at me, Storm once again pointed out my lack of extraneous exercise.

"I'll let you know Mr Sporty, I'm way more flexible than you. Now unless you want to eat cold food go shower up. I already have your clothes ready for you on the bed."

"Thanks, Doc, you're awesome." Lightly pressing a smooch on my cheek, I turned red all over again.

Storm was utterly dismissing my parents' presence and being his usual sweet touchy self. High fiving my dad and Kyle and boldly pressing a firm kiss on my mom's cheek, Storm thunderbolt the females of the house.

"Start your breakfast, Ang. Don't wait on me." He voiced out before walking out of the kitchen.

"I had no intention to." Grasping hold of my shock state, I quickly called out to his departing figure.

I wasn't his wife or girlfriend to be waiting for him to have break-fast. Yet, pondering over it, it dawned on me how much we both have the habit of waiting on each other. Be it for breakfast, dinner or even sleep.

"You two sounds and looks like a happily married couple com-pletely in love. - Don't they look like us during our first year of being married, Auden?" Staring deep into my soul like she was trying to pull my soul out of me by its collar, my mom remarked.

"Absolutely, Elize. If I didn't know any better, I would have guessed they were married for at least a year."

Ignoring my dad's unnecessary comment, I matched my mom's stare halfway and realised she was reaching. But she wasn't going to get a confession out of me any time soon.

"Does this mean I get to strangle him in his sleep when he annoys me?"

Pouring Storm's juice in a fresh glass, I kept it beside his covered plate of food before taking my seat and going through my laptop. The work of a renowned scientist and researcher never dies. Not even on a Sunday.

"I don't know what sort of world you live in but please, leave my innocent wife out of it. I value my neck, sleep and life." Covering his neck with both hands, my dad jocularly commented.

"Why? You don't want me to strangle the life out of you while you sleep when you take pleasure in annoying me?" Fruitily sug-gesting murder, my mom lifted both her brows at my dad.

"People, people, this is a crime-free house. I have no desire to be investigating a family murder." Walking back into the kitchen and putting an end to their murderous jestings, Storm began shovelling food into his mouth.

"Blame your partner, she started it, not us." Pointing towards me, my mom effectively turned the conversation back on me.

"Hey, I'm just sitting here working and trying to enjoy my breakfast." Chuckling, I took another big bite of my toast.

Coming up behind me, Storm placed his plate beside mine and slid his arms around my waistline. Gingerly kissing me on the cheek, my body involuntarily rested against his broad chest, and my neck instinctively tilted in the opposite direction, giving his lips more room to travel.

My head was screaming for me to pull away. It was trying to point out Storm was being overtly intimate and touchy in front of my parents. Sadly, my body was weak to Storm's physic and amatory touch. He was a drug to my body. He intoxicated my blood and willingness to resist. And somehow, after last night, my resistance seemed to have fissured - threatening to break at any given time.

"I'll blame my partner later. For now, she deserves my appreciation and gratitude for making me such a great breakfast and preparing my outfit for the day. She always takes so much care of me." Squeezing me in his hold, his comforting aura enveloping me, I knew he was sincere.

"Your partner will take all the appreciation and gratitude she can get. So please, don't hold back." Musing, I played along while opening my work emails.

"I'm sure she would." Pulling a chair next to me, Storm worked at finishing his breakfast.

"Do you guys have any plans for today or is it just work for you two?" My dad inquired after a while of chatting merely with Storm.

"We are going to the fair this afternoon." Storm summarised.

"Actually, guys..." Glancing at them and the new email I just opened, the guilt was plastered on my face as bright as the moon during a clear sky.

"No... - Ang, come on, we had planned for today a month in advance... Look at Kyle's excited face. He's been waiting for this with eagerness." Reading my face like an open book, Storm practically whined.

It wasn't just Kyle who had been excited about today's outing. Storm has been over the moon at the idea of bringing Kyle to his first real big carnival with me. He was adamant we go as a family from day one. For some reason, even as a grown man, Storm was just as excited as Kyle, a five-year-old, to go to the annual carnival. Me, on the other hand, wasn't so fond of all the high rides. Why pay for rollercoaster when my life was already a free ride of a rollercoaster.

"I know Storm, and I'm really sorry. But I just received this invitation from Doctor Benoit for a speech this Tuesday morning, and I need to organise all my notes for the subject he wants me to talk about. Not to forget, we have a critical interrogation tomorrow, for which I want to double-check with one of my recent researches for a better perspective. I basically won't have enough time for both if I go to the carnival today."

"But, mommy ..." Tears forming under his lids, "I really wanted to go." Kyle sucked in a deep breath, the sadness on his face and the slight trembling of his lower lip immensely pulled at my heart.

At that moment, I felt like such a terrible mother. Like one of those selfish, narrow career focus and status craving mothers. Whenever did I become one of them? When did my attention and focus shift from what was the most essential thing in my life to a superficial need? When did love and family become less important in my eyes?

"I'm not saying you can't go, Kyle. I'm just saying I won't be with you. You, Storm, grandma and grandpa can all go and have tons of fun. But mommy has some pressing work to finish. - I'll even let you have as much candy as you want for the whole day if you go with the flow."

Reaching over the counter, I grabbed Kyle's hands into mine. Pondering over my words and studying my encouraging smile, Kyle finally nodded his head in agreement.

"Good boy, Kyle. Mommy loves you." Smiling brightly at Kyle, I tried not to let the fact that I was choosing work over fun time with my son hover over my head.

"That's so not fair, Angel. I can't believe you are choosing Doctor Benoit over me again." Discerning the darkened look in Storm's eyes, I recognised he was irked.

"You are not being fair, Storm. You know how important maintaining a cordial relationship with Doctor Benoit is. His initial analysis on how to measure the changes in the peripheral nerve by combining electromyography of a muscle with electrical stimulation of the nerve trunk that carries fibres to and from the muscle is the core of my research on electroneurogram. With his scrutinisation insight, I am going to be able to work on my theory of directly visualising the recorded electrical activity of neurons in the central and peripheral nervous system. So, if he wants a few speeches of my renowned personality traits and microexpression link in return, then so be it."

"Who's Doctor Benoit?" Noticing the sudden dark air between Storm and me, my dad tried to break the tension. But miserably failed.

When Doctor Benoit is in the picture, Detective Storm Ives doesn't think straight. Not since he found out, Benoit and I have slept together on several occasions.

15

"**A** French guy with whom the Doctor here has more than just a *'few'* speeches and an unnecessary amount of pleasantry with." Storm venomously spat out.

"I get you don't necessarily like this French Doctor Benoit." My mom cautiously summarised.

"What's not to like about him? He's French, a well-known Doctor and has what Dr Angelica Buar desperately wants in his fist."

"He is just another scientist like me, mom. We met last year at a convention in France. He is currently doing some research work at another university in the city."

"Don't forget to add he's your little boyfriend." Clearly, jealousy had clouded Storm's judgement. He wasn't thinking straight anymore and was spitting out nonsense without any control.

"I went out with him on three or four occasions, Storm. That's it! Nothing more is going on." And clearly, I was getting exasperated. This new research was significant and expensive, I couldn't afford to flunk it.

"Elize, Auden, correct me if I'm wrong but if someone is done with someone else, as your daughter is exclaiming, would the person still be meeting up with the other individual for pleasantries?"

Sharing a look with each other, "Oh no, don't bring us into your couple fight." They simultaneously voiced out their retreat in our battle.

"Don't you pull my parents into your craziness."

"Okay fine, I'll pull you into my craziness."

LAVINIA DASANI

Fire against fire, we pierced each other through our mere gaze. The deafening silence around us, making my parents and Kyle uncomfortably shift in their seats. However, I was too mad to care about them right now. Storm was my sole focus.

"Room, now!" Closing my laptop with excessive force, I jumped out of my seat as did he.

"Excuse us, guys." Looking at the three in front of us, they seemed grateful to not be involved in our fight any longer.

Pulling the strong man by the arm, I pushed him inside my bedroom and locked the door behind me. Ferociously glaring at Storm with a flaming storm within me, I wanted to blaze him on fire.

"What the hell is wrong with you?" Threateningly marching towards Storm, I shoved him on the chest. To my annoyance, he didn't even move an inch. He stood there, glaring just as sharply as before.

"A lot of things is wrong with me." Grasping my wrists and clutching on it, he pulled me forward.

"But what the hell is wrong with you? We've had this day planned out for an entire month, then your little Doctor Benoit shoots you an email, and you're ready to drop everything. As if the first time you hooked up with him wasn't painful enough, you just gotta do it again."

"God damn it, Storm! It's just a scholar speech at a university. It's not like I'm gonna go there, give my speech and let him fuck me on the classroom table."

"No, maybe you'll let him fuck you on the floor or even go to his place and have wild sex. Or better yet, fuck each other -"

Cutting him off the only way I knew how, without having to smack the daylights out of him, I pressed my lips against his and kissed with force. Stumbling back with surprise, Storm fell onto the bed. Kissing him with frustration, exasperation and anger, he returned the kiss with the same fervour but with an addition of jealousy.

Hooking his legs into mine as I lay on top of him, I flicked my tongue into his mouth. Holding onto his face, I could literally taste

109

his jealousy and hunger for me. Lowly growling like an animal into my mouth, I moaned in response and further deepened the kiss. Letting our tongues dance in a beautiful tango of desire, need, want, ownership, possessiveness and love, the wall around my heart fell like a broken glass of red wine.

Feeling him grow against my throbbing core, a sudden realisation of the love in our actions, past and present, flashed in front of me. I was trying to deny the truth all these time, but at that moment when my mom's words of us looking and acting so much as a happy, loving married couple echoed in my head, I could no longer deny the truth.

I have been in love with the man for a long while now, and even if I wanted to build that wall around my heart all over again, it would be useless. I would just be going into an endless circle of destroying and constructing. Feeling my lungs constricting, I had to think twice if it was because I had just come to the most obvious conclusion of my life or because my need for oxygen was surpassing my desire to devour Storm's lips.

Forced by my body to break apart, my head felt lighter, and my vision blurring. Heavily heaving, I took in some much-needed air. Locking his green eyes into my darkened brown ones, I knew now was the time. As crazy and as badly timed as it was.

"What's wrong with me is I love you."

"You can't do that to us. The carnival is really important to Kyle and me - WHAT!"

As if now registering what I had said, Storm dumbfoundedly gazed at me. Dumbstruck, it was as if he was seeing an alien about to probe him.

"What did you just say?" Storm slowly spelt out his words in a low tone.

"I said there's something wrong with me." Taunting him, I purposefully avoided saying what he wanted to hear.

Storm himself has never directly said the 'L-word' out loud when we were alone, but he did say he enormously liked me. Additionally, his actions speak louder than his words.

"I know that. But the other thing, say it again." Playing right into

110

my hand, I loved seeing Storm writhe to hear the 'L-word' from me.

"I don't know what you are talking about?" Interlacing my fingers with his, I rode his hands above his head and inclined forward.

"Oh, do you mean how I admitted, I. Love. You." Sultrily articulating my words, I captivated Storm with my gaze and hold on his hands. Reading the pure happiness in his eyes, I closed my lips against his for a brief lip-lock.

"I love you too, Angelica. You have no idea how happy these words coming out of your lips makes me feel."

Holding his cheeks in my palms again, "Your eyes are a window to your soul, Storm. And from my position, I can see you are over the moon."

"Over the moon. Nah...... I would say, over the whole universe. After all, I've only longed to hear your acceptance of my love for roughly two years now."

Caressing his jawline and cheeks, "Oh Storm, I am sorry for making you wait this long. I'm not sure if I deserve this much love from you, but I am not going to hesitate to take your love anymore."

"You deserve so much more than what I am giving you, Angel. You are the most precious creation I've laid eyes on. I am just glad you have finally accepted us as an actual couple."

"I have accepted I love you and us officially being together because that's truly how I feel. Because of how long it took me to acknowledge this truth, I now know my love for you is more than real and not just lust. - But you also gotta know, I am still scared of relationship and what it brings with it. Then again, if my parents can stick together through thick and thin, I gotta believe there is more to love and relationship than pain and sadness. - And I wouldn't choose anyone else in this entire world to share this experience with. You've been there for me when I most needed it, so why not give us a shot and see where it goes."

Touching my cheeks with the back of his fingers, Storm lightly caressed my skin. "I know you are scared, Angel, but we will work through it, I promise. Just you giving us a chance is a big step forward. - Besides, I will be more than honoured to be your man even if most of your compliments were meant to butter me up so you could go meet Doctor Benoit without any hitch. On the other hand, I would also like to apologise for my insensitive attitude and behaviour. I do respect your work and understand how important it is to you. I was just so jealous, I wasn't seeing clearly. It killed me to know you were most probably going to be sleeping with him by the end of Tuesday... I just love you so much and can't bear the thought of another man touching you in such an intimate manner."

"I know, and I appreciate your apology. But know that even if you had disapproved, I would still have gone. This research project is way too important and has already cost so much."

"As long as you don't sleep with his French ass, I have no problem or worry."

"Storm, I just told you I love you. In this sense, I don't want any man other than you to make love to me. Let alone intimately touch me. But before we go any further, I want you to promise me you will drop your playboy acts and your other subs. No more fucking other girls while you are with me or we are done. - Are you ready to commit to only one person?"

Carefully studying him, I used all the skills I have learned through fieldwork and years of studying microexpression. I may be in love, but I wasn't stupid. There's no way I was gonna fall for another Dylan-move. I now had Kyle in the picture, after all.

"Angelica, you don't need to ask me twice. No other woman matters to me. For me, it's only you."

"Good, now that this is figured out let's get moving. You have a solo family trip to attend with my family, and I got work to handle. - I believe I'm leaving them in safe hands; especially since my parents know next to nothing about this city."

16

"**B**abe, you're speaking to a first-class detective. There's no safer than that." Grinning brightly at me, I couldn't help but return his smile.

"I'm trusting this first-class detective to keep my family safe. But I'm trusting my loving new boyfriend to show my family an excellent time."

"I'm loving hearing myself being called your boyfriend."

Leaning forward, our lips only inches apart, "Well, dear boyfriend, when you come home tonight, we still need to discuss how everything is going to work out. Remember, I haven't been seriously involved with anyone in the last five years."

"Don't worry Doc, we will make it all work out. We are partners, after all. - And if you want to take it slow, we can do that."

Loving and appreciating how compassionate and understanding Storm was, I dropped my lips to his. Passionately kissing, this unique moment was filled with only love, desire, need and want. His hands running all over my back and stomach, mine streamed its way over his shoulder and chest, I considered his words. Did I want to take it slow?

Right on cue, I felt his member pressed against my core, and I had gotten my answer. Breaking apart, "If you remotely try to slow down our timing of when we are going to have full intercourse, I swear Storm, I will break up with you before you can blink." Breathing heavily, my voice hoarse, I made my point.

"Eager much?" Teasing me, Storm mischievously smirked, gripped my waist and ground my entrance against his shaft.

Sucking in a deep sharp breath, "I swear to God, Storm if you don't stop teasing me I'm going to straddle you and ride you like a pony. And I don't think my family outside wants to hear us."

His eyes darkening to a denser green, the grey completely disappeared, "Don't give me any ideas." He huskily uttered.

We were both apparently in heat and from the swirling emotions in his eyes he was considering dismissing the possibility of everyone hearing us just like I was.

Pressing one last kiss on his lips, I unhooked my legs from his and got to my feet. "If only you had considered bringing your gag ball with you ... You could be screwing me senseless right now." Winking at him, I watched as Storm inhaled a ragged breath. The images and ideas floating his minds more than visible in his expression.

"Once I break into your tightness and make sweet passionate love to you, Angel, I'm gonna make sure to punish each one of your teasing words and actions."

Absolutely relishing the idea of his warning, I felt like teasing him even more. I was crazy. My ass was still sore and red from last night, and I was already looking forward to another punishment.

"Then babe, watch me walk out of this room, back to my parents. Watch me swing my firm sore red ass that you ate, whipped, smacked and caressed last night. The same ass my boyfriend is gonna fuck and pound into so hard, my screams are gonna echo through the wall."

"Ugh ... Angelica Buar ..." Catching sight of him clenching my bedsheet before I sped walked out of the room, I knew I had gotten him. Storm was most probably miserably trying to regain control of himself and his hormones inside my room.

"You guys all okay now?" Glancing up at me from the couch, my mom inquired.

"We came to an agreement." Musing and letting my words float in the air, I was wondering if I should tell them they won or wait for later.

"Well, someone looks like they've won the world most priceless treasure." Cocking his brow at Storm who was finally making his way into the living room, my dad exclaimed with utmost curiosity.

"You could say that." Grinning widely, Storm truly seemed beyond the universe.

The knowledge I was the reason behind such immense happiness and smile made my heart skip a beat; bringing just as big a smile on my face. Frankly, I was ecstatic at the idea of making him happy. Of being his. Of sharing my life and Kyle with him at a deeper level.

"Okay, I'll bite. What's going on?" Peculiarly looking between Storm and me, my mom loudly gave up figuring what was happening.

From the small smile tugging at her lips though, I knew she had a feign idea. She has, after all, been feeding me endless stories of how she had met my father since last night. How difficult it was for her to recognize her feelings and accept the idea of loving my dad. The woman had even spent all morning in the kitchen endorsing her marriage and love life, branding me with all its grandeur and happy moments.

Knowing her calculating, almost manipulative manners, I had no doubt she did all those on purpose. However, even if I wanted to, I couldn't be mad at her. She was after all the reason I have finally been able to realize and accept my love for Storm. If not for her persistence and pursuant stories, I would still be denying myself the love of Storm Ives, and we would most probably be in a major fight right now, instead of being all lovey-dovey.

Lowering the volume of the TV, I took Storm's hand in mine and gently dragged him to the love seat in front of my parents. Squeezing Storm's hand once, "Well, we got news for all three of you." Running my eyes over Kyle and my parents, who were all sitting together, I watched the curiosity spiked up in their eyes.

"Storm and I have decided we are ready to take our relationship up a notch and see how well we will do as a real couple." Rolling each word off my tongue, I carefully and calmly informed them.

"She finally admitted she loves me and agreed to be my girlfriend." Storm cheerfully jumped in, his excitement and singsong voice the complete opposite of my composed self. The man was acting like a teenager who just got asked out on prom by his life-time crush.

"Finally!" Coming up behind my parents at the precise moment Storm was done with this outburst, Anastasia exclaimed. With a grin of her own, she appeared just as happy and gleeful as my parents and Kyle.

"No need to sound so relieved and excited." Wittingly reprimand-ing Anastasia, I simultaneously took in my parents' smiling faces and Kyle's wide grin plastered on his delighted little face. The boy's happiness was high as a kite.

"Are you crazy? I should be throwing a major party to celebrate you finally accepting being in love with Mr Hotshot over here." Plumping herself on the couch beside Kyle, "Seriously, what hap-pened while I was gone?"

Taking note of her chirp attitude after being gone the whole night, I was slightly worried about Anastasia. However, I pushed it aside for now. I was going to confront her later on.

"Oh Ana, you have no idea what all have happened while you were gone. But let's just say my parents' magic brought this mira-cle in me."

"Well, Elize, Auden, whatever you did, I wanna congratulate you both and thank you. I've been trying to shove some sense into your daughter's stubborn brain for the past year, alas, to no suc-cess." Fake bowing to my parents from her seat itself, Anastasia brought a small laugh out of everyone except me.

I didn't have a stubborn brain. I have a brilliant mind with an IQ above the average. I was the best God damn Cognitive Be-havioural Psychologist this State have seen. I just take a while to figure out what I want in my personal life.

"I gotta admit, it was all Elize's idea. She and her intelligence are incomparable in comparison to mine."

"I knew it! I knew all your storytelling was part of a bigger plan. - And I can't even be mad at your Machiavelli plan. Because if not for you I would have never come to terms with my true feeling for Storm!" Pointing my index finger at my mom, I exclaimed in as low of an accusative tone as possible.

Shrugging her shoulders, "What can I say, I'm formidable that way." My mom dared wink at me.

"Mommy does this mean Storm will stay here with us forever?" A bit too animated, Kyle jumped off the couch and stood in front of Storm and me.

Not allowing myself to be influenced by the hopeful glint in his big brown puppy eyes, "I'm sorry, Kyle, but this doesn't mean Storm will be here forever, not yet."

Watching his face drops, my heart took its own dip. "But, Storm will be here more than the usual. He will even stay over on more nights if you want."

Yeah, I was a total sucker for Kyle. - Sue me - He was my prince, and I could hardly see him disappointed.

"Yes, little man, I would be staying over even more now. Are you ready to share your mommy with me?" Lowering his head to Kyle's level, Storm connected with my son once again.

"Yes." Rapidly nodding his head up and down, I was almost afraid Kyle's head was going to pop off.

Stretching his hand out to Kyle, "Deal."

Taking Storm's big manly hand into his small tender ones, "Deal," they sealed my fate.

Whenever did I become a prized possession in both of my most favourite men's lives? That was something worth investigating if you ask me.

"When's the fair, again?" My dad interrupted these two business-men's moment.

"In about 45 minutes," I responded to them.

"We should probably start getting ready then." Standing up, Anastasia voiced out.

At that moment it dawned on me Miss Anastasia Riles has been wearing the same clothes as yesterday, which in itself told me a lot. Chirper like a hummingbird, smiling, plus the same outfit as the previous day - This girl had some last night.

"Anastasia, where have you been?" Hoping to dear God it wasn't with 'Asshole- Jackson', I nonchalantly placed her in the spotlight. I know they met up last night, but I was mentally praying she didn't stay with him all of last night and this morning.

"I - umm - Charlie's." Furiously blushing, the colour on her cheeks matching the colour of her red hair, Anastasia stuttered.

"Charlie? ... As in Geeky tall doughnut-eating Detective Charlie - the tech specialist of my team?" Inquisitively sharing a confused glance with me before staring back at Ana, Storm inquired. The surprise on my face matching his surprise tone.

"Uh-hum." Was all Anastasia muttered, but I wasn't having a simple throaty noise as answers. I wanted details. I wanted to know what the heck had happened while I was busy getting myself spank and belted.

"Oh no, girl? I'm gonna torture the details out of you." Standing to my feet with a wicked grin, I evilly rubbed my hands together.

"It was nothing really. We coincidentally met outside a coffee-house before I went to confront Jackson again, so he helped me out with my Jackson-problem. We began talking afterwards, and we ended up at his place. End of story." Rapidly summarizing, she glanced around; more specifically towards her room and the front door entrance, she stepped foot through a few minutes ago. But the woman was not running away so easily; not after torturing me so much about Storm.

Taking Ana by her arm, "Tell your big sister all about it..." Dragging her with me to her room, "What did you guys talk about? What did you say like that? Or better yet, how much and how loud were you talking?" Suggestion filled in my words and tone, I swiftly raised my eyebrows up and down for emphasize.

"You guys get ready. I will be helping Ana get ready for the fair... see you all in 45." Voicing out from Ana's room, I closed and locked the door without waiting for their answers.

We both had only forty-five minutes to recount all of what happened in each other life last night and no matter how surprising her news about Charlie will be, my first full real introduction to BDSM would most definitely rock her mind. It is still rocking mine, for crying out loud.

17

Ping

"I left a package on your bed. Wear it tonight." Reading Storm's text a second time, a smile sneaked its way on my lips.

"What is it?" I sent back, the excitement of our first real date tonight getting the best of me.

I was feeling like a teenager in love and heat all over again. This week had felt exceptionally long and strenuous. We spent the whole week working on Mrs Hearth case; interrogating Mr Hearth, his son, the psychologist Mrs Hearth went to, the doctor who first treated Mrs Hearth and ending up arresting the poor son for the murder. Not to mention giving my speech at Doctor Benoit's college, and combined with the high sexual tension between Storm and myself the entire time, I was more than ready to relax. All I wanted was to enjoy Storm's presence and warmth in an intimate and personal manner.

"Oh, you will soon find out, babe." Another 'ping' brought my attention back to the present and what was awaiting me.

"Is your new loving boyfriend texting you again?" Walking up to me in his lab coat and Zachary, his faithful monkey, perched on his shoulder, Daniel, one of my co-worker at the science lab at the University inquired with a cheesy smile.

Looking up at Daniel then at Zachary, the grin could not be wiped off my face. "Yeah. We are finally going on our first official weekend date starting tonight."

Did I forget to mention everyone in mine and Storm's world now knows we are a couple?

Storm made sure everyone was aware I was now taken by him. He freaking stood on the balcony of the second floor of the station on Monday, called everyone's attention and announced the news of our new relationship. On Tuesday, he sent over a dozen rose baskets to the University. Stepping inside my usually immaculate lab was literally like stepping inside a garden. It was like a piece of the 'Garden of Eden' broke off and fell inside my lab. Given Storm's outpour of affection and daily roses the entire week, I was forced to reveal to everyone in my lab that Storm was indeed my boyfriend now.

As much as I loved all the attention, affection and endless stream of love, I recognised I also had to put a stop to the roses. My lab was at cost, and there was only so much I could give away to the university population.

"Doc ... Yo Doc! I need the template for the brain scan we did this week." Waving their hands in front of my face, Daniel and his monkey, Zachary demanded my ultimate attention.

"Yeah, sorry. Diverted attention and all." Going through my filing cabinet, I took out the scans and handed it to Daniel.

"Better get it all out your system this weekend, Doc. We have another electroneurography experiment with a new test subject next week."

"Don't worry Daniel, I'm not going to mess with my own research because I'm now in love."

"I'm taking you up on your words, Doctor Buar." Turning his back to me, Daniel left with Zachary without waiting for my response.

For sure, I wasn't going to let this new adventure in my personal life influence my lifelong work in a bad way. I have been hustling too hard for the later. I am just going to need to readjust my flow. To balance both aspects of my life accordingly. In other words, I needed to call my mom and ask for advice before I screw something up and I loved Storm way too much for the latter.

"Hello mom, I'm in serious need of your help."

"Please don't tell me you forgot to pack your bag for your romantic weekend getaway? Cause all I'll pack for you would be lacy thongs and bras."

"MOM!" Furiously blushing, my mind started imagining my mother of all people packing my luggage for a sex-filled weekend. "Why you gotta be so crude?"

"Not crude, dear daughter. Just trying to make sure you finally get some." Hearing the slight snickering in her tone, I simply shook my head in disbelief.

"Don't worry mom, I will be getting a plentitude this weekend. What I need from you is advice on how to not screw up mine and Storm's new relationship? How did you successfully manage work, your relationship with dad and us without leaving a trail of destruction behind you?"

Conversing with my mom for over an hour when I should have been working on my statistical data staring at me through my computer screen, I gained a whole new perspective and level of respect for my mom. Not to mention pointers on how I can better manage my entire life. Sharing and comparing ideas, she made me realise how advantageous it was that Storm and I were already working together. It made my issue of time management and work-focus so much easier. I swear to God, having my parents here with me has been nothing but a major blessing in my life. I almost wish my brother doesn't realise his mistake and try to bring them back to New Hampshire.

~~ | | ~~

"I can't believe you bought me all these and kept it in the open on my bed."

Taking single pictures of each of the items from the package Storm had sent me, I texted him my disbelief. Thank the Lord I had the logic of closing the room's door before opening the infamous package.

Laying in front of me was a gorgeous lemon-yellow ankle-high slit chiffon dress with a deep cleavage. But this wasn't the disbeliev-ing part. This was the nice sweet romantic part. Beside the dress, on top of my bed laid a black mesh lace bodysuit corset. It was a beautiful piece with a delicate flowery pattern in the centre, run-ning from below my chest to the end of my stomach. At the end of the piece, a garter belt was attached to the sides of the panty line.

Next to what was supposed to be my underclothes for tonight was a pair of sheer thigh-high midnight black stocking, featuring dainty flowery pattern around the top. Inside the packaging box that still sat on the edge of my bed was a pair of black closed-toe stiletto. The heels so tall, I could kill someone with it in seconds.

Ping

"Did you find the small box in the bottom of the box?"

Perplexed by Storm's message, I sent a quick "I didn't" while searching for it within the colourful tissue papers stuffed inside the box. With how everything was presented and the items inside the box, I could tell Storm was making an extra effort. The man was so loving, I was emu and almost felt like tearing up.

This genuine feeling of tugging of my heartstring, however, switched from a loving source to a lustful one when the content of the small box was revealed to me. Resting flat on my palm in all its grandeur was a silver Bluetooth mobile phone control wireless bullet vibrator.

"Really." Shocked, I sent a simple text to Storm.

"I take it you found my special gift. - *Winked face* emoji."

"No duh. - *Eye roll* emoji."

"Wear everything I got you. I will check for each and every single items."

Taking a quick picture of the vibrator which I knew would be my worst enemy by the end of tonight, "Even this devilish thing?"

"Especially this devilish thing. It will be the second thing I will check."

"What will be the first thing?"

"You making the yellow dress look even more splendid. Now go get ready. I'll pick you up at 6. Love you - *Heart* emoji, several times."

"Love you too. - *Blowing kiss emoji*. I 'll see you in a few hours." Leaving my phone on my bed, I went to take a shower.

~~||~~

Picking my wallet clutch from my living room table, "You guys are sure you would be fine babysitting Kyle all by yourself for the entire weekend."

"Angel, we are your parents and have raised you to be this wonderful lady, haven't we?"

Not paying real attention to what she was saying, "Yes, mom, but Kyle can be a handful if you are not used to him. I could call Anastasia back from her little vacation or postpone my trip for later?" My mother instinct kicking in at the last minute, I was second-guessing my decision to leave for my little weekend getaway. The timing really wasn't impeccable.

"You are worrying too much. Just go unwind and have some fun." My dad jumped in, his tone literally trying to push me away.

"Fine. - Just... call me if anything happens, please." My eyes begging for their cooperation on this matter, I carefully studied my parents.

"Helicopter parent much." My mom mocked with an eye-roll.

"Mom. Dad." Giving them a pointed look and tone, I didn't find any humour in this situation.

"Okay, fine!" They simultaneously responded.

"Good."

Turning towards Storm, who was quietly watching mine and my parents interaction with a slight smile decorating his lips, "I'll go say goodbye to Kyle, then we can leave."

Aware I needed a Kyle-hug, "Sure, I 'll wait." Storm patiently stated.

18

"Ready."

Taking Strom's outstretched hand as soon as I was in front of him, "Yes."

"Let's get going then. We still have a chance to make it to the cabin restaurant before it's too dark." Returning my smile with his own, Storm got my heart racing again.

Bidding my goodbyes to my parents and making sure they had memorized all my instructions one last time, Storm and I finally left the suite.

"You look stunning by the way." Holding hands like a lifelong couple, Storm gave me a sideways glance as we walked to his Mercedes Benz SLS AMG.

"Thanks." Blushing like a ripe cherry, I was suddenly feeling timid.

Now that we were an official couple, his compliments as innocent or naughty as it might, causes a rush of shyness to course through me. Being in an actual serious relationship after five years was doing funny things to me; my body and actions. I was so nervous I felt like this date was the very first date of my entire life. I would even go as far as say, the reality of being in a relationship with someone as caring, loving, patient, funny, genuine, handsome and practically mouth-watering as Storm Ives still makes me speech-less.

"Woh!!" Jumping in my seat and nearly hitting the roof of the car, I yelped.

Why, you ask? ... Let's just say, Storm's monstrous torture device breathed life within me.

Buckling his seat belt, a devilish grin plastered on his face, "You've followed my instructions to the letter, I see."

Arming myself with sarcasm, "You didn't leave me with much choice now, did you? - Ahh!! ... Shit!" Yup, his weapon was working with excellent efficiency and motion.

"That's only level 2, love." Turning his smartphone's screen towards me, "I have up to level 10, and it only gets worse. At level 5 alone, I can make you orgasm hard in a matter of mere minutes ... So please, keep that sarcastic attitude-filled mouth of yours running. I would love nothing more than to have you rapture several times on our way to the cabin."

Glaring at Storm, an almost dumbstruck look washing over my face, I was tempted to purposefully be sarcastic and show attitude. Only one week of being in a relationship with Storm Ives and one whole BDSM session where I got to overcome just one of my fears and I could see the changes within me.

"You're an asshole." Blandly defying Storm, I was clearly looking for it.

Roaring his car to life and driving off to our destination to some secluded cabin reservation with a lake view a few miles past the city line, "You asked for it, Doc."

Swiping his phone screen, locked on the dashboard of his car, the dominant in Storm was battling for control. However, I could care less which side of Storm was taking over. My attention zeroed on the ticklish and vibrating sensation between my thighs as it picked up even more speed and ferocity, causing me to squeal once more.

Not allowed to touch myself throughout the entire car ride, I used the roof of the car, and the top of the grab handle for support against the high and low vibration Storm kept switching between. One minute my pelvic bones felt non-existent, clouded by a warm vibrating and hazy pleasure and the next, the blood flow to my clitoris felt so much more intense, it shattered me without any hesitation.

Quivering with yet another hard release, I was literally numb. - Rapturing in waves of pleasure five times in a row would do that to anyone. Breathing heavily and hard, beads of sweat rolling down my forehead, I was flushed. Burning, I was unable to feel my private parts and most likely sticky as heck.

"Did you have enough yet, or do you want to continue being mouthy?" Taunting me, Storm decreased the speed from an 8 to a 4.

Fierily glaring at Storm while catching my breath, "I - don't … know what you're talking about?" Inhaling another deep breath, "My mouth is completely fine."

My body was demanding for me to stop testing my limits, but I wasn't going to give up so quickly. Not when reaching level 10 of this dang vibrator was my own personal challenge.

Instantly jolting at the sharp vibration of the bullet, I shrieked at the increased speed. My throat parched from all the moaning and screaming I've been doing, I felt speechless as I crashed and convulsed against level 9 in no time.

"I know you've purposely been defying me, Angel, but if you really want the last level of this vibrator, you're gonna have to beg for it." Bringing the vibration down to level 2, the slow torturous stimulation was killing me more than the fast, hard and rough stimulation.

Regaining control of my breathing, "Can't you just give it to me." Excessively battling my eyelashes, "Please … pretty, pretty please."

Laughing at my lame attempt to avoid begging him for more, Storm was having way too much fun for my liking. But the jerk-face knew he had me at his fingertips - literally. One upward swipe and I would have what I most desired throughout this long car ride.

"That's not good enough, Doc." The asshole switched to speed 1, "Tell me in as much detail as you can; what do you want? And what are you willing to do for it?"

Twisting my upper half entirely towards Storm, "I want you to increase the speed to 10 because I am craving to experience more than what I think my body can handle. In return, I'll let you do to me anything you want and desire for the whole weekend."

126

"Now that's a deal I cannot refuse." Going up a hill, Storm spared me a glance and a wicked smile.

What the hell have I gotten myself into by proposing this deal? - A whole weekend at Storm's ultimate mercy ... Oh, my God! I don't know if I would be able to handle it all. But a deal was once again struck out of my impulsiveness and enormous sexual desire. For Pete's sake, I really got to start working on handling my sexual appetite for Storm Ives. It was seriously getting out of hand and extremely costly.

"Brace yourself, Doc." Storm's warning came as an instruction.

"No, duh! It's not like I haven't been bracing myself the whole time you've been switching level like a monkey in my lab who just got a new toy." Clearly, pointing out the obvious in my yearning state was a stupid move from Storm. Then again, I never said the man was perfect; just better than most men I've gone out with.

"Well, Miss Sarcastic, I didn't ask you to brace yourself for the vibration of the bullet between your legs. It was for an entirely different reason."

Ignoring his meaningful glance and the fact that I had just made a fool out of myself, "Oh! What is it then?"

"You will soon figure it out, on your own, Miss Know-it-all."

That devilish smile decorated his face again, "Storm? - WOH!" Swiping upward, he activated level 10, instantaneously stopping me from questioning him.

And then, I discovered in the worst way possible why Storm had asked me to brace myself. Underneath us was a highly rocky mountainous path as we got closer to our destination. The combination of the high sharp vibration from the bullet vibrator and the bumpy ride, where I was literally bouncing from my seat created one of the most intense sensations I've felt in my life. It was like I was getting roughly fuck and vibrated at the same time. While the sexual monster in me secretly loved the latter idea, I was too numb and stimulated to even think properly.

"Storm ... please ..." Shattering, I couldn't find my voice.

"Please what?" Purposely speeding up on the rocky road, Storm taunted.

From the sound of his voice and the glint in his eyes, I realized he chose this path on purpose. I wouldn't doubt if there was a perfectly normal well-made path to reach the cabinet he rented. Storm was being mean and torturous.

"Make ... -Shit! - Make it ... Stop ... please..." All these bumpings, jolting and vibrating were getting too much for my untrained body.

"First, ride your dress completely up."

"What!" Dazed and confused, I gawked at him like a hawk.

Was he crazy? I was asking him to do one thing, and he completely changed the subject and asked me something random.

"You heard me, Doc. Ride your dress completely up, or I make this jolting ride all the bumpier and impactful for you."

"Fine!" With shaky fingers, I did as instructed, no matter how weird it was.

Decreasing the device and car speed, "Good girl."

Seriously, I didn't know which was worse. The quick rough bouncy ride or the slow, bumpy ride. I could now feel each and every bump from the uneven rocky ground along with the reverberation of Storm's monstrous object inside me. To top it off, Storm nonchalantly reached towards my thighs and planted his warm hand on my inner thigh.

"What are you doing? - And why isn't your torturous device off yet?"

"Patience, Doc."

"Not a quality I possess," I interjected.

What the hell was Storm plotting? Being in the unknown was playing tricks on my mind, and the controller in me was trying to poke its ugly head.

"But, one you will start to learn by the end of this weekend." Mischievously grinning and winking at me, there was no doubt Storm had something big plan. "Now, open your legs."

"What? Why? - Ahh! ... Fine!" That dang vibrator and its speed control; it was ferocious and merciless.

Slipping his hands between my legs, Storm forcefully pushed my panty line aside. "Shit!" I muttered under my breath the moment his index and middle finger stroke my clit.

Jerking at the intrusion, I literally didn't know what the heck I was supposed to do. From being stimulated by two factors, I was now being probed by a third factor.

19

"Storm..." I begged.

But for what? - For him to stop? To continue? - I was literally a clueless mess.

"We are about to arrive at the cabinet." Storm lightly informed me.

Arriving at the cabinet was the least of my worries. The gentle stroking of his two fingers, the slow bumpiness from the road, level 4 of his vibrating bullet and the way my body was reacting was my major worries right now. "And?" I breathed out.

"I want you to take my hand and dive my fingers inside you. I want to see you masturbate with my fingers the entire way; go around, beside or underneath the vibrator - I don't really care."

"Are you for real right now?" Disbelief coursing through me, this new form of request took me by surprise.

Quickly swiping upward with his free hand, "What do you think?"

"You're serious ... just ... please go down one level." Taking in my pleading eyes and tone, Storm finally cooperated and swiped back to level 4.

Placing my hand on top of his, I arched my hips forward and directed his fingers inside my core. Moaning, I started off slow, bringing his fingers in and out as my body adjusted to his two fingers. With tension building up without much hesitation, I pushed him further into me and rammed his fingers with greater force and speed.

As new as fucking myself with Storm's fingers while having a vibrator stuck up my vagina and the rocky road aiding in bumping my body against the sheer force of me pushing Storm's fingers inside of me was, I had to admit, it was fun. It was exciting in its own way. Not to mention, the orgasm was even more earth-shattering than before. By the time we finally reached the cabinet parking area, I was exhausted, on fire and sticky.

Breathing heavily, like I had just run a marathon, I was now looking even more forward to what Storm had in reserve for the entire weekend. I knew there would be a hell lot of bondage and smacking; Storm was, after all, a dominant. But what I didn't realize was how it was all going to play out.

Then again, having known Storm for a couple of years now, it was inevitable that our first time actually sleeping together would be vanilla, and I was super excited about that part too. What I was dying to know was the when, how, what and where. Not knowing the timing of it all was slowly killing me - or rather, killing my controlling side.

Removing his fingers from within me and licking all my juices off, "You taste wonderful. Like always."

Pulling my panty line to its original place and lowering my dress, "I can't wait until I can have my mouth on your sex."

Dropping my mouth at Storm's outspoken statement, I didn't get much time to respond back. Getting off the car, he came to my side and opened my door like the true gentleman he was.

"Thanks," I mumbled out of habit.

"Here." Handing me a pair of keys, "For the green cabinet on your left. Go freshen up, then join me at the reception. I'll go fill out all the necessary forms and have one of the luggage-guys bring our bags to the cabinet."

"Okay. But please tell me we are going to eat right after I freshen-up. I'm starving."

"How about I make sure setting up our table by the river bank takes priority."

Reaching for my face, Storm plastered a gentle kiss on my forehead. "I promise by the time you are out, everything will be ready for you to be served. It is an open banquet tonight."

"Perfect. I feel like I could eat a house."

"Get going then." Shooing me away, Storm lightly pushed me in the direction of the green cabinet.

"And Angelica, keep the vibrator on." With a naughtiness clear as the blue sky in summer, Storm had me shaking my head in disbelief.

~~ | | ~~

Strolling along the river pathway, hand in hand with the faint summer night breeze caressing my bare arms and face, I had to admit our first dinner-date was fantastic. The food was delicious; worthy of a five-star restaurant in the big cities and the desserts were so damn mouthwatering, I just had to stuff myself with it.

Being the extreme foodie, I just couldn't bring myself to care about proper lady-food-etiquette. I was way too hungry for the later. On the other hand, there was no way I would lack energy for a whole night of extraneous activities.

Carrying my heels in my hand, Storm and I enjoyed the quietness of our surrounding. The only sound we could hear for miles was the soft waves from the glittering lack. Hiking up my dress to my calves, I gently kicked the water; disturbing this beautiful sea of glimmering diamonds. And despite its crisp, freezing temperature, I found the water flowing under my feet to be appeasing. It cooled my warm body in an instant.

"What's on your mind?" Staring at me in endearingly and with a smile on his lips, Storm curiously asked.

"I'm just thinking about how perfect tonight was. I never imagined going out on a date with you would be so relaxing and fun."

I truly was surprised. With all the pent-up sexual tension between us, I had always thought going out with Storm will be a day filled with sex and well, any sort of fun that would lead to sex. Not that I objectified Storm; I just really craved the man. He was like alcohol to an alcoholic. One that obviously didn't need healing or intervention. All I needed was a release from all the tension inside my lower belly.

A tension created by Storm's monstrous device throughout dinner.

Thankfully he only switched the vibration back and forth level 1 to 4 the entire time. As a matter of fact, the vibrator was currently running on level 1 in this intimate walk of ours.

"I kept telling you we are good together, but you and your stubborn self never listened to me."

Jokingly chastising me, Storm actually made a pretty good point. If I hadn't let my fear of being hurt; of commitment and of relationship blind me, Storm and I would probably be celebrating our 2nd anniversary as a couple right about now.

"But at the end of the day I came around, didn't I ?" Going on my tiptoes and looping my arms around Storm's neck, I brought his head forward and pressed a firm kiss on his forehead.

"That you did. Even if it was in the most unexpected way possible."

"Better late than never." Taking in Storm's smile, I cheekily stated.

"Thank God for that." Bringing our interlaced fingers to his lips, Storm laid a gentle kiss.

Kicking the water again, causing droplets to fly in front of us, "So, what do you want to do next?" I nonchalantly tried to find out our agenda for the entire weekend. The secrecy of it all stroking my compulsive need to know everything in advance; to be in control of my environment.

I couldn't believe how ironic my situation was. I am the psychologist who was assigned to Detective Storm, to help out on his criminal cases and keep an eye on him, yet, here we were. It is Storm who has now turned into the psychologist and is trying to fix my psychological problems.

Abruptly stopping midway of kicking the water again, I let out a small whimper. "Storm! ... I asked what we were doing next, not for you to increase the vibrator's speed. - What level is it on? ... 3 or 4?"

My body already conditioned to not orgasm as quickly as before, I was able to speak without breaking, or singing like a canary. If you ask me, that's a great achievement. I could now handle more than I could only a day ago.

"But babe, I just answered your question in the most blatant way possible." Swiping upward on his phone screen, the inside of my body contracted and I knew we were now on level 5.

"Pleasing you is what we are going to be doing next."

Clasping hard on Storm's hand around mine, "Storm!" Was all I could manage to mutter.

Standing in the middle of nowhere, with a high-powered vibrator between my legs was so much more difficult than sitting in the car and driving to the middle of nowhere.

"Walk to that tree over there." Pointing at the tree a few feet away from the river pathway, the dominant side of Storm made its appearance.

From there on, I knew the vanilla side of Storm wouldn't poke its head until the time of us making love came. Without arguing, I slowly walked to my right, towards the tree he pointed, halting only a few times when he increased the speed and intensity of the device.

As much as I wanted to scream at Storm for making me walk with a vibrating bullet; to throw all caution to the wind and take any punishment he might give me, I was walking on uncharted ground and digging a hole for myself was out of the question.

Turning on my feet once I stood against the tree, I waited for Storm's next instruction. Instead of talking, though, he prolongedly sauntered to me. Capturing me in his gaze, Storm devilishly smirked and up the level somewhere close to ten. Looking at him with wide, pleading eyes, I was ready to crumble to the ground.

Gently unfisting my fingers around the strap of my heels, Storm took it from my grip and softly kept it on the ground. My hands free of any baggage, I instantly put it above my head and grasp as much as I could of the trunk for support.

"God, Storm! - Please..."

Hearing my pleas without much fuss this time around, Storm decreased the speed back to level 1. But then he did something somewhat unexpected given our environment.

Crouching down to his knees, he lifted the skirt of my dress, "Feel free to scream, moan and whimper as loud as you want. I don't want an ounce of restraint from your voicebox, reaction or action."

134

And disappeared under the skirt of my dress.

As much as I wanted to, I couldn't see him. All I could do was sense him spread my legs; his lips trailing upward to my inner thighs and see the outline of his head move underneath my dress. Having changed to a lacy G-string from the lacy panties that had gotten soaked and sticky from my many orgasms, I was suddenly grateful.

With the thin strip spreading my ass cheeks when Storm pulled upward on it, I realized a G-string was the most appropriate material in our current situation. With a regular panty, he would have had to remove it, and I would be missing out on the marvellous pressure the stretched thin strip of the G-string was applying on my throbbing clitoris.

Licking the base of my G-string that had further spread my clit, I nearly came, right there and then. But I held onto my verging orgasm, waiting for it to build to a much higher intensity. Just like the time in my room when Storm had me handcuffed and didn't allow me to cum until he said so.

Sensing him shift my underwear to the side, the thin strip laid on top of my butt cheek, leaving me entirely bare for him. Running his mouth and darting tongue all over my dripping womanhood, it was like his tongue was running a lap, and my sex was the course.

Gently pushing my arched hips back against the trunk, I moaned and whimpered in pleasure. Writhing under the incredible attack of his talented mouth, I found the back of his head and pushed him deeper into me. The way Storm was nibbling on the bundle of my nerves reminded me of when I was eating those mouthwatering desserts earlier tonight.

And it would appear I was a delicacy he just couldn't get enough of.

20

Looping my arms around Storm's neck, I pillowed my face on his broad chest and allowed myself to be carried bridal style inside the cabinet. The comforting warmth his body was emitting calming my racing heart and tingling body. His strong hold cocooning me in a layer of protectiveness, like a parent's wings of protection would around her child.

Gently laying me down on the soft mattress of the king-size bed, Storm stood by the feet of the bed and peeled off each layer of his clothing with the slowness of a snail. Gulping in anticipation, I watched like a hawk, not daring to avert my eyes from his scrumptiously jacked self.

Dominant Storm long gone, the reality that we were going to experience our first lovemaking tantalized my senses and the sweaty sensation in my palms returned with its own excitement. After 2 years of craving and dreaming of this lecherous moment, time seemed to go slow, almost like it was going to pause on me. Butt naked, Storm climbed on top of the bed and advanced towards me like a moth to the flame. Inevitable.

Hovering above me, the grey outline in his eyes entirely overtaken by the green, his longing for me was just as intense as mine; if not more. Caressing my lips with his, I gave Storm my all and plunged into his slow and sensual intoxicating kiss.

Locking his neck between my arms, I freely roamed my fingers through his tangled hair and explore his mouth with my tongue. Taking his time like he was kissing me for the very first time, I was quickly spellbound. Swiping his tongue around mine, his hands roaming to the zipper of my dress, I arched my back even further, eager to get this dress off me.

Smiling at my impatience, Storm broke the spell and bore his lustful eyes onto mine. "Tell me you love me, Angelica." Gingerly shedding my dress from my body, Storm requested. Not once removing his attention from my eyes.

"I do, Storm... I love you." Reaching for Storm's face once the dress was thrown onto the floor, I cupped his cheeks and brought his lips back on mine.

"And right now, you are the drug that's keeping me from dying." I mumbled against his lips before slowly sliding my tongue into his mouth again.

Responding to my delicate kiss, Storm's hands skimmed along my flesh, leaving a trail of warmth in its path. Blazing from the inside-out, I was itching for Storm to rip off the lacy corset and G-string, and ravage my body the same way his mouth was devouring my mouth.

"I love you, Angelica." Kissing down my collarbone and cleavage, Storm peered up for a beat and divulge with utmost love and passion.

"Me too..." I purred at the delirious assault of his lips and tongue onto my skin.

Flaring with ardour, I was more than thankful when Storm finally peeled off all my clothing despite his claims of how much he loved seeing me in all those laces. I had to admit, the man had great taste in women lingering. The lingerie he had chosen for me, was not only beautiful but also accentuated my features and fitted me like a glove. The dark colour of the laces decorated my body, embellishing the colour of my skin and gave me the allure of a Sexual Goddess.

Nudging my legs apart, I was more than ready to receive his sheer power of potency inside my throbbing self. My chest heaving beneath his mouth and touches, I was left wide-open for him. But Storm being all about patience when I didn't have any ounce left, took his sweet time massaging my thighs and decorating my body with his smooches.

"Storm..." I whined between laboured breaths. I had enough of his playing around. I wanted him inside of me, and I wanted it now.

Proudly and mischievously smirking at my eagerness and appetite for me, Storm grabbed my hips and pulled me closer to him. Teasing my entrance with his hardness, Storm grazed my vulva several times, increasing the anticipation and my need for more.

"Please, Storm... I want it...." Not caring how exposed I was, I moved my hips around, trying to get him inside of me.

"If you want it, then you shall have it." Smiling, Storm mused.

Wrapping my long legs around his waist, Storm slowly plunged inside me, his length taking up all the space. Burking my hips at his repeated deliberate evasion, my moans were loud and unstoppable. Our 2 years of restraint finally becoming undone, I was more than elated to relish in this beautiful moment of slow lovemaking.

Interweaving my arms under his, I firmly clutched onto his shoulders, as my inside clasped around his thrusting length. Taking my lips into his, Storm effectively muffled my cries of pleasure and picked up his speed. Beads of sweat rolling from my temple, I unravelled underneath Storm without any care in the world. All that mattered to me at that moment was him and me interlacing in this hot and sweaty amourous venture.

Sweating and flaring with arousal I lost myself into Storm's lovemaking to me and my body. Hearing the grumble of his ecstasy as he relentlessly thrust into my welcoming womanhood turned me on to the next level. Convulsing under him, the explosion within me detonated and shattered my composure. Screaming out in zealousness, I saw stars and touched heaven.

Falling on my back with a *'pouffe'*, I could have passed for a putty. Kissing me on the forehead, Storm rolled off me, "That was so much better than my dreams." With a wide smirk, so gorgeous, I wanted to capture to stare at forever, Storm vociferate on his way back from the jug of water sitting across the room.

Taking the glass of water from his hands with a grateful smile, I jugged it all down. With the amount of blissful screaming I've done today itself, I was surprised my throat hadn't completely given up on me yet. Thankfully, I had a guy who knew just what my body needed when it needed it.

"You. Have. No. Idea." I mumbled, sipping the last drop of my heavenly water.

Taking my glass from me, Storm refilled it, "Here. You need to hydrate. - What we have coming is going to be far more intense and exhausting." With a wink, Storm kept the jar of water on the bedside table.

Wolfing down my drink, the wits in me poke its head, interested to know more. "What do we have coming, sir?" With absolute innocence, I batted my long eyelashes at Storm.

Sitting down on the edge of the bed, next to me, Storm's eyes smouldered, my teasing getting to him. Brushing the back of his fingers along the line of my face while I drain my glass of water, "We are going to have a little impact play."

Swallowing hard, the wittiness in me said its *'bye-bye'* and I was left open-mouthed. Unclasping the glass from my hands, Storm gently placed it on the bedside table and moved away from me. The mischievousness in his eyes, clear as daylight.

"Do you know what kind of cabin this is, Angelica?" With an eerie air, Storm asked.

Looking up at him through my lashes, "No, Sir." I had originally thought it was like any other vacation cabin around the state. But the look on his face told me a whole different story. There was indeed something special about this place - about this cabin.

"This camping ground is not your typical ones. It is owned by the BDSM Club I am a part of."

My breath hitched, just at the mention of that place. I remember the owner of that BDSM club. He was so powerful. So gigantic in all shapes and forms. And the way he held himself..... It screamed danger. Heck, the man was on the far extreme side of the BDSM spectrum, and the air around him demanded for everyone to bow down to him - to worship the ground he walked on.

But Storm Ives didn't. He met him head-on. Confronted the high-powered man with his own high-octane personality. At that time, I couldn't begin to comprehend how these two dominant and puissant men didn't tear each other apart from the moment their eyes crossed. It wasn't until later, after the mission that I found out about their friendship.

139

Capturing my attention by opening the wardrobe, "And each cabin has been specially made for a BDSM session. We have anything
and everything we need here, just like in the dungeon."

Slanting forward, I tried to peek inside the cupboard. Sensing my
curiosity, Storm moved to the side, leaving the wardrobe wide
open. My breath stuck in the back of my throat, I could swear my
eyes practically bulged out of its socket.

In front of me were arrays of different sizes and shapes of whips,
floggers, paddles, restraints, and ropes hung on the back wall.
On the left door of the wardrobe, all sorts of handcuffs and mask
were attached. There were all variety and style; from fluffy pink
to leather to black metallic cuffs and eye masks. The right door, on
the other hand, was decorated with collars. From the most colourful to the blandest ones. Some were spiky, while some were as soft
as cloth; maybe even silky.

Slightly squinting my eyes from the bed, I was left baffled at the
words and name-calling written on most of those callers. Briefly
looking between Storm and the multitudes of collars, especially
the ones with 'Bad Kitty', 'Slut', 'Cumwhore', 'Kitty', 'Slave', among
others, written over it, I seriously hoped he wouldn't have me
wear any of those. I loved the man, but I wasn't one of those submissives, nor desired to be one.

"Why don't you step closer? There's so much more inside here
you haven't even seen yet." Holding his hand out for me, Storm
instructed in his least dominant tone.

Swallowing, I walked up to Storm, each steps oddly feeling
heavier than it should. Running his eyes all over my naked body,
the excitement within them calmed my nerves to a certain degree;
however, part of me was still scared of the unknown ground I was
walking on.

Taking my hands in his, Storm wrapped his arms around my
waist, planting my back against his well-defined chest. Feeling
every part of his front against my back, the butterflies within me
woke up from their slumber. Picking interest at Storm's touches
and his hunkiness.

Release the hold on my hand, Storm opened up a cupboard inside
the wardrobe, his hot breath tantalizing my senses. Making me
boarder on brain dead. **Almost.**

After seeing the exposition of gag balls and nipple clamps, memories of all those subs gagged, with clamps on splintered through my brain. My throat suddenly dry despite all the water I drank, I ogled at the exhibit staring point-blank at my face. From nipple clamps with feathery bottoms to metallic, well intricate designed bottoms, the cupboard had it all. The one with the silver metal butterfly bottoms, hanging on small metal loops, attached to a black bow that then attached to the clamp, however, was the one that really caught my attention.

Looking up to the several toys, specially designed for impact play, the icicles glass anal plug with a flogger affixed to its end, entranced me. The palm of my hands itched to touch it. Especially the leather flogger hanging from its post-derrière.

Reaching out, and taking the plug down, "I see you like this one." Playing with the tip of the icicle, Storm gruffly stated.

Twisting my neck and glancing up at him, I simply nodded. Caressing my ass, his soft yet rough palm created friction so delicious, the wetness between my legs happily let its presence known. Closing his lips to my right ear, "It will soon be used on you." Storm huskily stated.

"Yes, sir." With staggered breaths, I just agreed to whatever at that moment. The mere idea of Storm using both the flogger and the plug on me, causing my heart to pick up.

Smiling by my ears, Storm knew in that moment, I was basically uncontrollable and was willing to try anything with him. "Pick whatever collar, handcuffs and eye mask you want. A gag won't be necessary." Biting down on my earlobes, "I love hearing you scream way too much." Pinching my left nipple between his fingers, a moan left my lips.

Glad Storm didn't force his choice of restraint on me, "Yes, sir." Not letting my creeping blush affect me, I chose the red leather wrist restraint for my cuffs, red eye mask with black embroidery laced on the edges and a simple red leather collar, with small black holes decorating the material.

"Good girl." Taking my restraint for the night away from me, Storm directed us to the bed again.

With the slowness of a snail, Storm clasped the collar around my neck. Picked up the wrist cuffs and tethered my hands in its leathery trap. Grabbing my fastened wrists, Storm tested the cuffs by pulling my hands apart as much as the metal connecting the restraint would allow him. Happy with himself, he bore his eyes on me, the seriousness as real as it could ever be.

"You're ready."

Realizing full well, Storm wasn't just asking if I was ready to be roughly fucked, but was in reality really asking if I was genuinely prepared to submit. To follow his lead to the letter. "Yes, sir." With confidence, I wasn't aware that I possessed for this type of unknown venture, I let Storm know I wasn't backing down.

Kissing me on the forehead, "Good." Storm muttered before sliding the mask over my face, stealing my sight in a snap.

21

Draped in utter darkness and restraint, my sensory senses kicked in, heightening the effect of Storm's breaths, touches, kisses and strokes. All I could do was stand still, let Storm direct my body as he deemed appropriate and enjoy. Just enjoy. Nothing else.

Kneeling on the soft mattress, my ass up in the air, my inside sweltered and my breathing was refusing to let go of its death grip around my trachea. Clutching harder on the pillow underneath my head, I didn't need my eyes to know Storm was running a Wartenberg wheel along the outline of my back and over my buttocks.

Carefully mapping my ass cheeks to perfection, like he was drawing the world's most intricate map, the sensation of the metal pinwheel was unique. Dangerous if not appropriately handled. But absolutely exhilarating if used with the right precision. And Storm knew just how to use this medical device.

Sensing Storm's lips on my skin, so close to my butt hole, yet so far away, I was itching to just grab Storm by the back of his head and push his mouth into me. To feel his tongue deep into me. To end this slow torture of his smooches on my flesh.

"Sir..." Practically wiggling my behind into his face, I pleaded for more contact. But Storm..... Devious little Storm ..... Wasn't having any of it.

Feeling his smile against the skin of my rear, I knew Storm was going to be relentless. And by the end of this night, I was going to become the queen of begging.

Disappearing from behind me, the lack of Storm's warmth sent a chill down my back. Staying in position as instructed, despite hating being left like this, unable to see my surroundings and basically just trusting Storm and his intentions, goosebumps ran across my body.

"Lay on your stomach." Hovering above my body, Storm ordered close to my ears.

Curious as to what he was going to do next, I crashed my body on the mattress without any hesitation. Trailing his hot kissing from the back of my neck down to my calf, Storm caught me off guard when he clasped another pair of cuffs around my ankle.

"Sir?" The need to know what was happening or what he was planning, killing me, I couldn't keep my questions buried any more.

"Shush... Just trust me." Keeping my arms separated above my head, Storm vocalised. The Dom in him mixing with the sweet version of him.

Nodding, "Okay." I mumbled.

Tying a leathery strap on my wrist restraints, I tried to tug, but couldn't go very far. I was left arms apart. Somehow bond to the bed.

"But, can I at least know what you are doing?" Totally ignoring his instruction to just trust him and enjoy this moment, I inquired.

Spanking my post-derrière in one brusque movement, "I said no more questions." Spreading my legs apart, and swinging at my stinging butt cheeks again, Storm was fully immersed in his dominant character.

"Sorry, sir." Hissing at the spanking, I apologised and let Storm work on attaching another pair of straps around my ankle cuffs.

Sprawled on my belly, spread like an eagle in an 'X' formation, I found myself unable to close my legs or hands together. No matter how much I tugged at the leathery ropes affixed to my leather cuffs, there was no escaping my restraint. **I was indeed at Storm's complete mercy.**

"Jerking won't do you any good, Doc. You're attached to this wonderful little system called, under-the-bed restraint and no matter how much you yanked at it, it's gonna keep you in whatever position I want, for however long I want." Dragging his fingertips along the wetness of my vaginal opening to my rear end, Storm informed me in a calm and cogent tone.

With no vision, all I could do was sense his touches, his breaths, the power of his words and imagine. Imagine what it must be like to look down at myself, sprawled and restraint. With ragged breathing, my pool of desire increased as the images of what I must currently look like and the hungry, lustful glimmer in Storm's eyes as he devours me with his mere gaze, flashed in front the darkness surrounding me.

Unable to close my thighs or clench myself around Storm's fingers as he stroked my beads of pleasure, no matter how much I pulled at the restraints, my juices of need flowed free. Sensing the icicle glass tip of the anal plug brushing against my womanhood, swamping into my juices like it was a river, I took in a deep breath and arched my hips as much as the restraint would allow.

The fire within me blazing, the throbbing between my legs was demanding to be put at ease. Aching with needs and literally feeling like I was going to die from Storm's continuous tortuous grazing of the plug from my vagina to my butt hole, "Sir, please..." I begged. The shame I would have felt a weak ago wholly incinerated in the burning fire ravaging inside me.

Placing a firm kiss on my bottom as a response, Storm slowly slid the icicle plug inside my bum, lubricated by my wetness. Hoarsely moaning at the intrusion, it took my body a minute to fully adjust. Lifting my hips a few inches from the mattress, Storm brought back his devilish egg vibrator and turned it on to level 3 inside of me.

"Your old friend wanted to say hello." With his broad smile caressing my face, Storm teased.

Burking my hips, the intensity of the vibration now far more torturous and vibrant, "It's no friend..." I hissed between ragged breaths. "It's ... an enemy..."

Upping the level, "Say that again."

"Still... not my... friend." Ignoring the soft caress of the whip's leather tails against the skin of my ass, I wheezed.

145

'Swish'

Yelping at the sting of his several lashes, I fell back onto the bed. The sensation of the vibrator and plug curving deeper into me, bringing me close to ejaculation.

"Do you know what type of whip I am holding right now?" Whispering dangerously close to my ear, I gulped at the dominance in Storm's voice.

"No, sir." I really didn't. All I knew was that it had several tails and it stung like a bitch.

"It's a 5 fingers whip; one of the evilest, with five tapered and hand skinned fingers of fire." Caressing my stinging flesh with the tapered again, "So, babe, I would be really careful with the demonstration of attitude."

"Yes, sir." I muttered.

"Good girl."

Sensing Storm placing the whip down on the bed, "But, sir ..... it's still not my friend..." I declared, my demonstration of attitude, as he put it, very much alive.

"You're just looking for more smacks, aren't you."

Storm didn't laugh. His tone was still dangerous. But I knew he was smiling. I knew he found it funny and was absolutely bemused by me and my wittiness. And that on its own was hugely satisfying for me.

Hissing at the smack against my flesh, "No, sir." I uttered with innocence so pure, even the angels would have been jealous.

Increasing the vibration's level and flogging my ass with a plain leather one tail flogger, the triple sensations were driving me nuts. Fervently searing, I grasped hard on the straps binding my cuffs, afraid I would fly off the roof at any minute, and plain out scream my lungs out in pleasure and pain.

Shaking under Storm's incessant stinging hits, numb from the sharp vibration inside my vestibule, the blood flow to my clitoris so much more intense, I burst apart. At that moment, I couldn't be controlled. I was a convulsing mess. Pain and pleasure mixed together, I had no idea which one had the upper hand. Nevertheless, if I had too, I would do it all over again. The intense crashing my body just went through was out of this universe.

Catching my breath, I didn't give a damn about what Storm was doing. But, I guess, I should have.

Prying the anal plug away, Storm grabbed onto my hips and pulled me into him. My breaths stuck in my lungs, I was left open-mouthed when Storm rammed himself deep inside my ass hole. Gurgling as Storm took me from behind, pounding onto me like a raging animal and upped the vibrator to a 10, I just couldn't. I was beyond a mess and definitely up in smoke.

Exploding like a rocket taking off in no time, "Storm...... I ..... I ..... need... to breath....." Falling flat on my face, I was spent, and my throat was screeching for rest and water.

Turning off the vibrator and pulling it out of my convulsing body, "You did great, baby." Storm reassuringly pronounced before placing a firm kiss on the back of my head.

My body still shaking, cum still rushing out of my anus and vagina, I closed my hooded eyes and simply nodded my head at Storm. The caring undertoned in his dominance propelling my already rapidly beating heart to skip a beat.

Untying my legs and hands, Storm sat me upright and removed the mask from my face, giving me my sight back. Slowly opening my eyes, I allowed my vision to readjust to the lighting. Coming face to face to Storm's piercing smouldering gazes, I gave him a weak smile.

"Here, drink."

Gleefully taking the glass of water from Storm's hands, I relished in the cooling effect of the cold water against my dry throat. "Thanks," sucking the last droplet of water, I mumbled.

Sitting beside me and stroking my thighs, his gentle touches causing my heart to flutter, "No problem, Angel." Storm spelt out.

Laying a gentle kiss on my cheek, "You were excellent and as much as I would love to try all my toys on you tonight itself, I know I've exhausted you."

Keeping the glass back on the bedside table, I rested my head on Storm's shoulder and engulfed myself in his warm, comfy hold.

"That you have."

Laying us down and pulling the covers over us, I pillowed myself up on Storm and relished the quietness and calmness surrounding us.

"I'm glad we came here." Tightening his hold around me, Storm kissed my sweaty forehead.

"Me too, Storm." Yawning, the sleep trying to get to me, I mumbled.

"I love you, Angel." Bidding his goodnites, Storm divulged.

"Me too, Storm. I love you." I sleepily muttered, the darkness of sleep already gripping onto me.

EPILOGUE

"I can't believe I'm getting married again." Stepping into my white chiffon wedding dress, I was mesmerised at how gorgeous and perfectly fitted the dress was.

With a lacy off-the-shoulder neckline, this tight sheath of white fell around me and train on the ground. The chiffon veil attached to the back of the neckline, it almost enveloped me like a superhero's cape.

Zipping me up, "And I can't believe it took you this long to say yes." Ms Elize Baur, as always had to be her sarcastic self.

"Up top that one." Chucking another glass of wine and ignoring my raised eyebrows, Anastasia wholeheartedly agreed with my mom.

"You're lucky I don't have another bridesmaid, Ana." Allowing the makeup artist to finish decorating and accentuating my face for the day, I taunted.

"Indeed, I am. Can you imagine having one of your lab partners helping you be all girly while not mentioning a single scientific word for a whole week? - No, I didn't think so." Embellishing her rose long strapless ruched bridesmaid dress with a teardrop diamond necklace, Ana mused.

"Now, now, ladies. Let's not start a competition." Bringing her attention back to Ana and me, after having instructed the hairdresser what she should do with my hair, "Let's just be happy Angelica is marrying a charming, loving and great man. My daughter definitely deserves it."

"Thanks, mom." Blushing at the mention of the man I was finally marrying, my heart skipped a beat.

Even after two years of seriously dating Storm, a part of me was still bewildered. And when he popped the life-changing question two months ago on our official 2nd anniversary, I was awestruck. But also ecstatic. Unlike my past self, I was no longer afraid of commitment, and when the question arose, my *'yes'* came without any hesitation.

Knock *Knock* *Knock*

"Who is it?" My mom took the one out of my mouth.

"The bride's ring boy." My father answered for Kyle.

Chuckling at my father's attempt to mimic a child's voice, my mom opened the door for him and planted a light kiss on his lips before allowing them in. Running straight towards me with excitement, Kyle beamed like the ray of sunshine he was.

"You look beautiful, mommy." With pure happiness spreading across his face, Kyle looked up at me like he was looking at a Goddess.

Cupping his face and pressing a light kiss on his cheek, "Thanks, sweetheart. You look handsome, yourself."

Blushing, Kyle threw himself at him. Catching him in my arms, I managed to keep both of us stable on the chair I was occupying.

"Kyle, sweetheart, you are scrunching up mommy's wedding dress. And you, young lady, you are putting your makeup all over him." Slowly detaching Kyle from me, my mom stated and gently wiped my lipstick off of Kyle's cheek.

"We all need to remain presentable until this wedding is done." She practically scolded both Kyle and me. Raising one of my delicate eyebrows at her, I bit down on my sarcastic remark. The woman has been helping out with this wedding since day one, after all.

"Yes, grandma."

"Yes, mom."

Kyle and I simultaneously uttered.

Sitting Kyle down on a chair beside me, "You got the ring, Auden?"

Rolling his eyes at my mom's compulsion to control everything, "Yes, hun." He affirmed in a tone that confirmed my mom had asked him this specific question once already. If not more.

Chuckling at them, I looked at myself in the mirror, the reality of what I was doing entirely settling in. Dressed like the perfect bride from one of those expensive wedding catalogues that promise everlasting love and happiness, I was ému.

I was aware it won't always be sunshine and rainbows with Storm, especially with him being a dominant, but most importantly, because of our highly dangerous and stressful life. There will definitely be raining seasons, even stormy and snowy ones. But after being in a relationship with him for 2 years and working together to overcome ninety per cent of my fears and most of his, I realised we will be okay.

We were a team from the very start, and after tonight, we will be a stronger team and family. Looking at my parents through the full-length mirror, I knew we will all be okay. And, I certainly couldn't wait until Storm and I become more like my parents. Still loving, teasing, respectful, and a team even after so many years of being married.

"Ana, you and Kyle need to walk out in five minutes. Angelica and Auden, you two follow after a few seconds. Just like we practised last night." Looking at her wristwatch, my mom ordered, taking over for our event planner again. By now, I'm sure the poor lady was ready to rip out her hair in frustration and just hand over her job to my mom. Thankfully, I didn't have to break up a fight in my wedding dress.

"You're ready for this." Taking hold of my shoulders after everyone left the room, my father softly inquired.

Boring my eyes on his loving ones, "As ready as I would ever be." Breathing out, and getting a handle on my shaky legs, I felt like a teenager who was going on her first prom with the guy of her dreams.

"You got a good man there, Angelica. I'm happy for both of you." Kissing me on the cheek, my dad sweetly vocalised.

Smiling, I didn't have to say anything. I indeed had a good and loving man. Storm Ives was basically prince charming. But with a tint of kinkiness and a love for making me scream with deliriousness.

Hands in hands, my dad walked me down the aisle of the church, his radiance slowly killing off my nervousness. My regard fixated in front of me, Storm's genuine bright smile and amorous gaze welcomed me and instantaneously murdered whatever nervousness was trying to take over my body and mind.

Beaming at Storm, I slowly walked down the aisle, images of how we first met and all the adventures we've had since; good or bad, flooding my mind.

"I'll trust you will take great care of my daughter." Giving me away, my dad muttered in a low voice for only Storm and me to hear.

Taking my hand in his, the love and hunger in his beautiful eyes very much alive, "The day I stop, Auden, is the day I'm dead." Passionate as ever, Storm strongly muttered. The power in his words, causing my heart to skip a beat.

Running my gaze all over the scrumptious piece of heaven that was Storm, I couldn't have been happier. In his 3-piece royal blue suit that suited him to perfection and black bow tie, Storm was picture-perfect of a Greek God. If this man weren't already going to be mine, I would have been jealous of the bride.

"Don't drool too much." Closing his lips to my ear, Storm teased before getting back to his position.

Yup. This was the man I was marrying. A tease, corky, dominant, loving, caring, passionate, possessive, but most importantly, sincere and truthful. A partner I could always count on to watch my back.

Clearing his throat, the pastor gained all of our attention. Undivided, I took in every single word and every second of the moment. Grinning like a Cheshire cat as he passed the wedding ring through my finger, I knew that unlike with Dylan, I was bound to Storm until death does us part.

Meaning every word of my vow to him, I bound Storm to myself. The excitement of our adventure for our future selves bubbling inside of me. Sealing this contract of love, companionship and family with a kiss, I knew from the depth of me that I would never get tired of the dominant and caring Storm Ives.

As Storm always says, we were made for each other. And our past shaped us to the extent that we became more than compatible. We were two pieces of puzzles that click perfectly.

****

THE END

ACKNOWLEDGMENT

Writing this short erotic novel has indeed been an experience. Especially with it venturing in a space that is often frowned upon. But it was one that taught me a lot.

I want to say a special thank you to those people on my twitter and Instagram that have indirectly helped me gain more knowledge about the BDSM world and how it works.

I was fortunate enough to have befriended a few people who are involved in this world, and who have even got as far as writing their own books on the subject of BDSM.

The friends/acquaintances I've made on this journey have majorly helped me refocus my erotic writing when I felt like I was out of ideas. - You know who you are, and a big thank you to you.

My fans and readers, you are not forgotten either. I realize this book is a bit different from my usual writing, but I hope from the depth of me, you will enjoy this novel and the plot.

I wanted to write so much more on this one, but I figured I shouldn't cramp all my sexual ideas in one book. Primarily with this being a short story.

Again, a major thank you. I wouldn't be able to do what I love without you and your support.

READ MORE FROM LAVINIA DASANI

✖COMING NEXT✖

THE SPY WITHIN – BOOK 1 OF TAME SERIES

Calm Cold Collected and Controlled Federick Ashton Archer meets Fiery Sassy Brazen and Wild Phoebe Ziva Smith in the least expected place. What started as a curious interrogation turned into something more in the worst time. Get lost in a funny yet drama-filled novel, where two worlds collide. - A world of spies and business billionaires.

UNMASKING – BOOK 2 OF TAME SERIES

'Drop the mask and revel in the beauty of being bare'... The only instruction Phoebe Smith has to adhere by in her new odd, out-of-norm friendship with Federick Archer.

Then again, will this new instruction really allow Federick to take on the almost impossible task of unmasking Phoebe's dark secrets?

Will Phoebe be able to cope with the whirling fire that is her life, or will she finally crumble under the pressure surrounding her?

ABOUT AUTHOR

Lavinia Dasani is a psychology student and an author of Provocative Action Romance and Contemporary romance. She is a writer with a sassy and playful attitude. The things she loves the most are; travelling, planes, reading, fashion, and animal- especially horses.

Even when she is busy writing, she enjoys connecting with her readers.

Learn more and connect with Lavinia Dasani:

Website: laviniadasani.com

Twitter @DasaniLavinia

Facebook.com/Lavinia Dasani

Facebook.com/LaviniaTaming

Instagram.com/Lavinia_dasani

Snapchat @d_lavi1

www.ingramcontent.com/pod-product-compliance
Lightning Source LLC
Chambersburg PA
CBHW051947170626
46808CB00007B/2523

9781733985734